ECHOES ACROSS THE SNOW

A Trapper's Story

DJ ATKINSON

MW01515970

DJ ATKINSON

Copyright © 2024 DJ Atkinson All rights reserved
Some of the characters and events portrayed in this book are based on
real people and situations. Most parts have been fictionalized to varying
degrees, for various purposes. All of the dialogue is purely fictional.
This is a work of fiction. Names, characters, places and incidents either
are the product of the author's imagination or are used fictitiously.
No part of this book may be reproduced, or stored in a retrieval
system, or transmitted in any form or by any means, electronic,
mechanical, photocopying, recording, or otherwise, without
express written permission of the publisher.

ISBN: 9798879882377
Imprint: Independently published

Cover design by: Art Painter
Library of Congress Control Number: 2018675309
Printed in the United States of America

For DJ Reid

For the coffee, the quiet,
and the calm beside me
as the words found their way.

DJ ATKINSON

PART 1

DJ ATKINSON

1

Seattle's docks were an iron lung, breathing in cargo, exhaling commerce. A city within a city—wood, steel, sweat—its arteries pulsed with the rhythm of ship horns and chain clanks, the grind of wheels on damp planks. The scent of brine and tar thickened the air, and the morning fog, rolling in off the Pacific, veiled the ceaseless toil in a shifting cloak of gray.

Samuel Hawkins moved through it like a force of nature. A man carved from the docks themselves, broad-shouldered, thick-handed, his presence loomed in the mist, steady as the tide. To some, he was a cornerstone—strong, reliable. To others, he was a threat, a challenge to the fragile hierarchy of men who scraped their living from the sea's edge. Respect came in two forms on the docks: admiration or resentment. And for every man who nodded in quiet acknowledgment of his strength, another watched him with narrowed eyes, fists tightening around rope or steel.

Among them lurked Eddie Clark. Wiry, sharp-eyed, his presence slithered between stacks of cargo, his mind as quick as his hands. He had once imagined himself the man others would follow, but this man, without seeking it, had stolen that place. Where he was overlooked, the other was acknowledged. Where he was tolerated, the other was needed. Envy festered in the marrow of his bones, sour and relentless.

That morning, as the fog curled thick over the docks, his bitterness took form.

A timber load.

Not just weight. Leverage.

It hung suspended by rigging that had borne countless tons before. But not today. Not after his hands had worked the knots, weakening the sinews that held the massive beams in place. The sabotage was precise, measured—not a reckless snap, but a slow, inevitable unraveling. The moment would come when his target stood beneath it, a calculation of timing and fate.

The ropes groaned.

The morning hummed with the sounds of labor, oblivious to the malice woven into its machinery. He watched from the periphery, every creak of the timber load a note in his silent symphony.

Then, the unraveling began.

The ropes frayed, a betrayal disguised as accident. The timber did not simply fall—it swung, a pendulum of ruin, its descent masked by the shifting fog.

The dock seemed to pause, as if the world itself had caught its breath.

But the giant moved.

Not with hesitation, not with panic, but with the instinct of a man who had lived his life dodging danger. A sidestep, a shift of weight, and the timber load crashed where he had stood seconds before, splintering the dock with a force that sent tremors through the planks.

For a moment, silence.

Then, voices rose in a wave—shouting, cursing, the scrape of boots as men converged. The saboteur stood among them, his face carefully composed, the relief of failure buried beneath a practiced mask of indifference.

His fingers flexed, slow and deliberate. "You saw it." A pause. A chance. Someone—anyone—to say otherwise.

The foreman met his gaze, unreadable. "Loads slip all the time, Sam."

Eddie smiled. "Yeah. Accidents happen."

The crew murmured, tension loosening but not disappearing. He exhaled, slow and measured, his fists still coiled at his sides. He wouldn't push it—not now.

But as his adversary turned, offering one last smirk, he knew this wasn't over.

And the other man, despite the momentary victory curving his lips, knew it too.

The docks had a way of settling their own debts.

Samuel left the docks without a word. The salt air clung to his skin, thick with the scent of damp wood and oil. He walked fast, his breath heavy, his hands flexing at his sides. By the time he pushed open the tavern door, his pulse had steadied, but the fury had not.

The tavern smelled of sweat, whiskey, and regret. A dim-lit sanctuary for dockworkers, where exhaustion pooled in the bottom of every glass. Conversations murmured low, a steady drone broken only by the occasional clink of glassware. The air hung thick with the weight of men seeking solace—or the next fight.

He found Eddie easily enough—slouched at a table, eyes glassy with liquor, a grin curling at the corner of his mouth like a man who'd just gotten away with something.

He leaned in. His voice was low, steady. "You think I don't know it was you?"

A lazy look up. "Prove it, big man." He swirled the

amber in his glass, his smirk widening. "Seems like your muscles don't grow brains."

The space between them tightened. Conversations dimmed, the air thick with anticipation. The men around them, seasoned in the language of impending violence, edged away.

His hands curled into fists. One breath. Another. Then that smirk.

The chair scraped back, and he swung.

Fists met bone. Wood splintered. The fight was swift, brutal—a hammer to a rotting beam. When Eddie finally crumpled, the only sound was Samuel's breath, heavy and measured, filling the space where the scuffle had been.

The victory felt hollow.

He turned, pushing through the onlookers, stepping out into the cold night.

The air bit at his skin, sharp and bracing. He leaned against a brick wall, lighting a cigarette with unsteady hands. The flame flickered, casting momentary light on his face—jaw tight, knuckles split, something restless churning in his chest. The smoke curled into the darkness, carrying the remnants of his anger with it.

From inside the tavern, laughter resumed. Glasses clinked. The world moved on.

But Eddie's voice cut through the night.

"This isn't over. You'll regret this."

The words, slurred but certain, hung in the air like a rusted blade.

Samuel said nothing. He watched the door, waiting. And when it creaked open, spilling warm light onto the damp street, he staggered out.

Their eyes met.

A moment stretched. The tension between them thickened. A glass broke inside the tavern.

Then, a step. A stagger. A wheezing breath.

He went down.

No gasps, no screams. Just the wind slipping through the empty street, a stray dog trotting through the alley, the slow, steady retreat of footsteps.

Samuel stood over him. No turning back now.

Seattle was no longer his. The docks, the men, the sweat-stained camaraderie—it had all turned to ash.

East.

Butte, Montana.

He walked. Past shuttered windows and gas-lit streets, past the dockyard smoke curling like fingers at his back. The city did not stop him. It did not see him. He was already gone.

2

T he Bennett farm sprawled across the Iowa plains, a patchwork of fields and fences stretching to the horizon. A world of soil and sweat, where the earth dictated the rhythms of life —the rising sun marking toil's beginning, its descent signaling exhaustion's reward.

Ethan Bennett had been born into this rhythm, raised in it, shaped by it—but never at home in it. At twenty, he was tall, broad-shouldered, his hands calloused from years of work, yet he felt himself a stranger in his own skin. His body belonged to the farm, but his spirit yearned for something beyond the rows of corn, beyond the creaking barns, beyond the weight of expectation that pressed on him like the unrelenting summer sun.

Nights were his reprieve. When the day's labor was done and the house fell silent, he sat by the glow of an oil lamp, immersed in pages that spoke of distant lands, grand ideas, and lives untouched by soil-stained hands. He traced the words with his fingers, imagining a future where his hands wielded a pen instead of a plow, where ink, not dirt, marked his palms.

But dawn always came. The dream always dissolved. And the farm always pulled him back.

Each morning, he walked into the fields, the damp earth clinging to his boots, the cornstalks rustling in the wind like whispers of a life that would never be his. He moved through the motions—pulling weeds, mending fences, tending livestock. The air was thick with the scent of hay and manure, the sounds of labor filling the spaces where silence might have allowed thought.

His father worked beside him, a man hewn from the land, his face lined by the seasons, his hands thick with the memory of years spent coaxing life from the soil. To him, the farm was more than land; it was legacy, duty, survival. And his only son was meant to inherit that burden.

"The land provides for us. Always has, always will," he would say, voice edged with something between warning and plea. "Ain't no future in dreams."

He never answered. Not in words. But his silence spoke volumes.

Between them stretched an unspoken war. The books

were a betrayal, an insult to everything built with hard hands and sweat. The farm was a cage, and the man who worked it was its warden.

His mother understood. She moved through the house with quiet grace, her hands soft where the other's were hard. She had once been like him, he thought—full of longing, full of unspoken wishes. But the farm had claimed her, too. And so, she soothed where his father burned, offering small mercies in the spaces between arguments.

"He only wants what's best for you," she would say. "Even if he doesn't know how to show it."

But what if staying meant suffocating?

The questions festered. And then, one blistering summer afternoon, the answer came in the form of fire.

The thresher roared and rattled, its iron teeth devouring the field. He should have been watching it, but his mind had wandered—lost in the tattered pages of '*Around the World in Eighty Days*', a borrowed escape into a life of adventure.

The rock was small, unnoticed. The machine swallowed it whole. A screech, a shudder, a plume of smoke. Then, flames.

Fire spread fast in the dry fields. He moved before thinking, grabbing a burlap sack, beating at the flames. His father was beside him, movements sharp, desperate. "Goddammit! Don't let it reach the barn!"

They fought the fire, but the wind carried it forward, turning golden wheat into black ruin. Smoke stung his eyes, burned his throat. His arms ached, his breath came in ragged gasps.

Too late. The fire won.

By the time the flames choked themselves out, the field lay in ruin—ash and embers where prosperity had once stood.

The silence was worse than shouting. When it finally broke, the words were jagged. "This is what you were doing?" A boot nudged the remains of the book, half-burned, barely recognizable. "While our farm burned?"

He swallowed, chest tight. "It was an accident."

"An accident?" The laugh was sharp, bitter. "Your damn books mean more to you than this family! More than our future!"

Something inside him snapped. "What future? Breaking my back in these fields for the rest of my life? Living in the same cycle, watching the years slip by? That's your future, not mine!"

His father's face darkened, fists clenched. "You think you're better than this life? Too good for the land that's fed you?"

"I never wanted this life! I never wanted any of it!"

The words cracked between them, final as the charred remains of the field. The anger burned hot, but beneath it, something deeper. Something unspoken. Disappointment. Loss.

And he knew. Knew that nothing he could say would mend this. Knew that he had to go.

That night, he packed his few belongings into a battered suitcase. The room that had once been his world felt small now, a shell he was shedding. His mother lingered in the doorway, eyes red, hands trembling. "Are you sure?"

"I can't stay, Ma." His voice was steady, but his heart ached. "Not after this."

She nodded, lips pressing together, as if holding back words she couldn't bear to say. Instead, she reached into her pocket, pressing a few folded bills into his hand. "It's not much, but it'll help you get started."

He hesitated, then took it, knowing it was more than money. It was permission.

"Where will you go?"

"Butte. There's work there. A newspaper needs writers."

A sad smile ghosted across her lips. "A writer... you always did have a way with words."

She hugged him, her embrace a silent plea to be careful, to be sure, to never forget where he came from.

When he stepped out into the night, the farm stretched before him, its fields blackened by fire, its fences still standing. He looked back once—saw his mother in the doorway, saw the barn where his father's rage still simmered.

Then he turned away.

Each step carried him further from what had been and closer to what could be. The road to Butte stretched ahead, unknown, uncertain. But it was his.

For the first time, he was free.

3

The house stood on the edge of town, a weary structure that seemed to shrink beneath the weight of the mountains. Colorado's earth was scarred with the remnants of a dying industry, the town once pulsing with miners and saloons now fading like the last embers of an abandoned fire. The air carried the scent of iron and dust, the ghosts of prosperity lingering in the cracks of boarded-up windows.

Inside, the walls whispered of better days. Floors creaked under the shuffle of tired feet, the air thick with the weight of unfulfilled aspirations. A family moved through this space like shadows, each caught in a silent battle against time and circumstance. The youngest of four, seventeen and already hardened by a life of scarcity, James Morrison had grown up in this slow unraveling, watching hope wither into something brittle, something that cracked under the pressure of survival.

His father had not always been this way. Once, he had been strong, a man of sinew and steel who found pride in the labor of his hands. He had walked home from the mines with the kind of exhaustion that spoke of honest work, a provider who had built a family with quiet certainty. But the industry that fed them had begun to die, and with it, so had he. A slow descent —first the layoffs, then the odd jobs, then the bottle. A man who had once commanded respect was now a ghost of himself, his strength curdled into anger, his love drowned beneath whiskey.

His mother had been different once too. There had been laughter in her voice, a lightness in her step. She had married a man with promise, believing in a future that crumbled beneath the weight of disappointment. Over time, that warmth eroded, worn thin by fear, by blows, by the slow retreat into silence. She moved like a specter, tending to a home that had long ceased to be a refuge, her presence a muted force against the chaos that ruled within its walls. He—nearly a man —saw in her a reflection of his own fading dreams, a cautionary tale whispered in the way she flinched at shadows.

He had learned to move carefully, to gauge the air like a miner testing for dangerous fumes. His father's moods shifted without warning, anger flaring without cause, leaving behind bruises that ran deeper than the skin. The lessons came young: silence was

safer, distance was necessary, and love, if it had ever existed here, had turned into something twisted beyond recognition.

There were nights when he would wake, the scent of whiskey thick in the air, the shadow in the doorway more nightmare than man. The voice, low and slurred, would slither through the dark. "Close the door and lay down." Those words, a command edged in menace, had long since burned into memory.

Somewhere in the depths of suffering, something in him had hardened. He had learned how to mask the bruises, how to carry himself as though untouched, though the truth carved into his bones told another story. He had learned how to endure. But endurance was not enough.

The day came when survival meant escape. It wasn't planned—it was instinct, a moment where years of restraint shattered into something raw and uncontrollable. The words had hit their mark that night, insults hurled at the only person who had ever offered him kindness. His mother had flinched, stepping back, a silent plea in her eyes. The urge to protect her surged, but years of knowing better kept him frozen—until his father laughed.

Something in him snapped. He lunged, shoving with every ounce of force buried beneath years of restraint. The man stumbled, crashing into a chair, fury twisting his face as he bellowed threats.

He ran. The cold air struck like a slap, lungs burning as he put distance between himself and the place that had never been home. But fear did not loosen its grip, and after the rush of defiance faded, something heavier settled in its place. He had left her behind.

Hours passed before he returned, steps careful, body tense. The house loomed in darkness, quiet but for the low crackle of dying embers. He moved through the rooms like a shadow, driven by the need to know she was safe.

Then, the glow. A single ember in the dark—the tip of a cigarette, burning slow.

His pulse thundered. The silhouette in the chair shifted, the voice curling through the stillness. "You think you're a man now?"

He had no time to react before the figure rose, looming. The glint of a bottle caught the dim light, and he saw the moment before it swung. His body moved before his mind, hands grabbing for anything —anything—to stop what was coming.

The bottle turned against its wielder, shattering on impact. The man staggered, then crumpled. The silence that followed was different this time. No more threats, no more drunken slurs. Just the sound of his own breathing, ragged, uneven.

He stood over the body, waiting for movement, waiting for proof that he had not just ended

something irreversible. A groan. A shift. His father was alive, but unconscious.

And for the first time in his life, the fear was gone.

He moved quickly, hands steady despite the adrenaline coursing through his veins. Money from the man's pocket, the few things he could carry, the weight of years slipping from his shoulders with every step. In the kitchen, she stood in the dim glow of a flickering bulb, her figure fragile against the night.

"I have to go." The words came soft, final.

She did not meet his gaze. Her hands wrung the fabric of her dress, lips pressed together. When she finally spoke, it was barely a whisper. "You should have left a long time ago."

Something twisted in his chest. "Come with me."

She shook her head, the motion small, resigned. "I can't."

He nodded, the ache settling deep. He had always known the answer.

A few crumpled bills pressed into his palm. "Take this," she murmured. "And don't look back."

He stepped toward the door, then hesitated. "You deserve better."

She did not reply.

The night swallowed him whole. The air was crisp, the road stretching ahead long and empty. He did not know what waited beyond the horizon, only that it was not this.

Butte. The name had surfaced in overheard conversations, a place where men carved futures from rock, where a boy running from ghosts might disappear into something new. A town of miners, of movement, of stories waiting to be told.

He walked toward it, the weight of the past settling into the footprints he left behind. The road was uncertain, but for the first time, it was his.

4

The city pulsed with its own brand of darkness, an undercurrent of power and fear that ran beneath the surface of Chicago's bustling streets. William Donovan had spent a lifetime navigating its labyrinth, carving his name into the bones of the underworld. At forty-five, he was more than just a man—he was an institution, his reputation built on ruthlessness and an unrelenting hunger for control. But for all his cunning, for all the bodies left in his wake, true dominance remained just out of reach.

His rise had been swift. Not born from necessity, but from ambition. Never content to take orders, never satisfied with being a cog in another man's machine, he climbed through the ranks with a careful balance of brutality and charm, his mind always three moves ahead. His hands were stained with the deeds that turned small-time enforcers into legends, and he learned early that in this world, loyalty was a fragile thing—less a bond, more a currency, and one that could be spent or stolen in an instant.

Despite his wealth, despite the fear his name commanded, he chafed against the constraints of the hierarchy. The bosses viewed him as an asset, a necessary evil, but never an equal. Every step toward independence was met with scrutiny. His ventures—side hustles that lined his pockets and expanded his influence—were tolerated, but only just. He could feel the noose tightening, the wary eyes of the men above him watching, waiting for a misstep.

That misstep came not from carelessness, but from trust.

Vinnie had been at his side from the beginning. A man cut from the same cloth—sharp, ambitious, hungry. They had built their empire together, clawing their way to the top, their partnership a bond forged in blood and betrayal. But in this world, alliances were fleeting. The moment one man's ambition eclipsed another's, the knives came out.

The betrayal unfolded with meticulous precision, a slow unraveling that ended in fire and lead. The mob bosses, wary of his growing power, found their excuse when Vinnie whispered in their ears. His side hustles, once tolerated, became the justification for his downfall. The hit was sanctioned. The city that had once been his hunting ground turned against him overnight.

He had seen it coming. Not the specifics, not the players, but the inevitability. Power demanded sacrifice, and he had spent his life making others pay the price. This time, it was his turn.

In the shadowy confines of an aged speakeasy, hidden beneath the bustling streets of 1924 Chicago, the air was thick with smoke, the low murmur of jazz masking the weight of the meeting. Around the table, his men leaned in, waiting.

"Listen closely," his voice was a steady whisper, cutting through the ambient noise. "We've got a golden opportunity to shift the balance of power in our favor, but it's going to require precision, guts, and absolute loyalty."

Vinnie, ever the skeptic, tilted his head. "What's the play, Bill?"

He spread out a map, the city's arteries drawn in fine ink. "There's a convoy. Three trucks, loaded, coming in from Detroit. It's meant for Big Joe's operation—but it's never going to get there."

The men leaned in, the weight of the proposal settling over them. "We hit it here," he pointed to a narrow street, a known bottleneck perfect for an ambush. "We block the road, force them to stop. Quick, clean."

"And make it look like a hit from the North Side gang?" Vinnie interjected, his expression unreadable.

"Exactly," he affirmed, a glint of something ruthless

in his eyes. "We leave enough clues to point the finger at them. While the factions rip each other apart, we consolidate power."

One of the men flexed his fingers over his revolver. "What about the muscle riding with the convoy?"

"We go in armed, but this needs to be clean. No unnecessary heat," he said firmly. "Vinnie, you and Mickey on the snipe. Take out the drivers before they know what's hit them."

Vinnie nodded, his expression tight. "And the goods?"

"I've got a warehouse ready to stash them until things cool down. Untraceable to any of us."

The group murmured in approval. The plan was meticulous, every angle covered. He leaned back, leveling a measured gaze at his men. "Remember, this isn't just a heist. It's a statement. After tonight, Chicago will never be the same."

A silent pact formed in the dim light of the speakeasy. They weren't just thieves in the night; they were architects of a new order, ready to ignite the fuse of war and let the old guard destroy itself.

The deserted street lay in wait, swallowed by darkness. He sat behind the wheel of a nondescript vehicle, his men positioned in the shadows. The air was thick with the weight of anticipation. The convoy was coming. This was the moment that would shift the balance of power in Chicago.

Headlights broke through the gloom. Right on time.

Then, something was off.

Gunfire snapped through the silence—too soon, too much. Not just from his men. Another group. Unseen. Waiting.

An ambush on their ambush.

Instinct took over. He dove for cover as metal screamed, bullets cutting through the air. The attack was coordinated, precise. Not a rival gang. This was different. He scanned the chaos, searching for the face he knew had to be there.

And then he saw him.

Vinnie.

Not at his side. With them. Directing them.

Their eyes met. A beat of understanding. Then, the coward ran.

He took off after him, pushing through the chaos, ignoring the pain searing his shoulder. He reached the car, tires screeching against the pavement as he gunned the engine. The sedan ahead fishtailed onto a side street, weaving through the labyrinth of the city. He followed, adrenaline surging, fury fueling every turn.

Through alleys, down abandoned roads, the chase twisted through Chicago's underbelly. Every turn, every brake-light flash, tightened the distance between them. Then came the mistake—a sharp turn into a dead-end construction site.

He killed the headlights, rolling forward like a predator in the dark. There was nowhere left to run.

Ahead, skeletal beams stretched against the night sky. And there, waiting, stood the traitor.

"You set me up," he growled, stepping from the car, gun heavy in his hand.

The smirk was almost lazy. "You always thought you were the smartest in the room. But power? It demands more than just brains. It demands loyalty."

The word was a curse in his ears. "Loyalty? You wouldn't know it if it shot you in the face."

A step closer, emboldened. "Oh, but I do. I'm loyal to the winning side. And let's face it—you just lost."

He didn't hesitate.

The fight was brutal, a clash of betrayal and survival. A misstep, a stagger, footing slipping on cold steel. The smirk wavered. The balance wavered. And then—

Gone.

The silence was deafening.

William stood at the edge, staring down at the abyss that had swallowed the man who had once been his closest ally.

Chicago was no longer his city.

So he vanished. The open road stretched before him, leading to unknown destinations. Butte, Montana, was waiting.

5

Butte, Montana, 1925—a town carved from ambition and ore, where copper ran through the earth like veins of wealth. Once a beacon for silver and gold seekers, it had transformed under the rule of the Copper Kings, magnates who shaped the skyline with towering headframes and lined their pockets with the sweat of men who toiled below. The air was thick with the scent of earth and metal, the rhythmic clang of industry echoing through the streets, a symphony of progress and toil.

For all its prosperity, the town was divided. The opulent mansions on the hill overlooked the cramped, soot-streaked neighborhoods of the miners, whose bodies bore the scars of their labor. Immigrants from across the world filled the saloons and boarding houses, their languages and customs weaving together in a chaotic, vibrant tapestry. But beneath it all, tensions simmered. The promise of fortune clashed with the reality of exploitation. Strikes, whispers of union uprisings, and the ever-present danger of the mines kept the air charged with unease.

Into this world, men arrived seeking reinvention, redemption, or power.

James stepped off the train with nothing but a battered suitcase and the weight of the past pressing down on him. The town's energy was infectious, the streets alive with the clamor of miners, the rhythmic creak of saloon doors, the ever-present rumble of ore-laden carts. It was a stark contrast to the desolation he had left behind. Here, he could disappear into the throng, rewrite himself in the ink of industry and ambition.

Survival came first. He took what work he could —unloading supplies, sweeping floors, odd jobs that demanded nothing but sweat. The town, for all its opportunities, was unforgiving to those without means or connections. But he had a keen mind, a talent for listening, for watching. Secrets traded hands as easily as coins, and soon, he learned to deal in information. What started as casual observations became a commodity, whispered truths exchanged in darkened corners. He had found his niche, navigating the town's intricate social web, becoming an unseen force in the underground economy. No longer just surviving—he was building something.

Samuel arrived with ghosts at his back. The docks of Seattle had hardened him, but Butte was something else entirely. The weight of his past followed him through the bustling streets, a constant whisper that any face in the crowd might recognize him. The mines, with their relentless hunger for men, loomed as an option, but he hesitated. He had seen enough men broken by work that asked for too much and gave too little.

Instead, he took jobs that suited his size and presence —hauling supplies, working as a Bruiser in a saloon where fists spoke louder than words. He was a giant to some, a shadow to others, his mere presence enough to dissuade trouble before it began. The work suited him. He understood the language of hard men, the unspoken rules that kept a place in check. Each night, as he tossed out drunks and kept watch for trouble, he felt himself settling into this new life. Slowly, the paranoia faded. He realized Butte was filled with men like him, all seeking a fresh start, all burying past sins beneath the weight of honest toil. He kept his head down, worked hard, and for the first time in years, allowed himself to believe that maybe, just maybe, he had outrun his past.

Ethan arrived carrying nothing but the hunger for something more. The vast, unbroken fields of Iowa were a world away, replaced by the relentless churn of industry. The headframes towered like skeletal giants, and the streets pulsed with the ceaseless motion of ambition. Yet, amidst the movement, he felt untethered, a young man lost in the current.

It was by chance that he found himself at the doorstep of *The Butte Miner.* With no formal training but a sharp mind and an eager pen, he presented himself as a man willing to learn. The editors, perhaps recognizing the fire in his eyes, gave him a trial. He walked the streets as both an outsider and a chronicler, capturing the triumphs and tribulations of a town that refused to be tamed. His first stories exposed him to the raw divide between wealth and labor, the relentless spirit of those who toiled, and the iron grip of those who ruled. The farm faded into memory, replaced by ink-stained fingers and the thrill of shaping narratives.

Then there was William.

He arrived under the cover of both notoriety and anonymity. Chicago had been a battlefield, and he had left it behind not in defeat, but in calculated retreat. Butte was his new arena, its riches another empire to claim. He understood power, how it moved, how it could be seized. He studied the town, its players, its weaknesses. The Copper Kings had their thrones, but thrones could be toppled.

He did not start at the bottom. Instead, he found an opportunity—a mine on the brink of collapse, its owners drowning in debt. With the same precision he had used in the underworld, he offered salvation wrapped in a contract that left them with nothing. It was a ruthless maneuver, his first foothold in a town that did not yet know his name but soon would.

From there, his rise was methodical. Some rivals were outmaneuvered in boardrooms, others faced more direct consequences. Accidents happened. Men disappeared. His past in Chicago had taught him that power was not taken—it was built, brick by brick, deal by deal, whisper by whisper.

To the town, he was a businessman. To those who knew better, he was something else entirely.

And so, in Butte, these four men moved through the streets, their fates unwittingly weaving together in the shadows of the mines. A town built on copper, on ambition, on struggle—it would become the crucible where they would rise, fall, and collide.

6

The air inside *The Copper Vein* was thick with smoke and the weight of unspoken deals, a place where ambition clinked against glass rims and promises dissolved as easily as whiskey on the tongue. A muted hum of jazz curled through the dim-lit space, threading between murmured conversations and the occasional burst of laughter that never quite reached the eyes of the men who frequented its shadows.

William sat at the bar, his gaze moving over the room with the patience of a predator. He wasn't looking for a mark—he was looking for potential. And there, nursing a whiskey in the low light, he found it.

The man had a presence. Broad shoulders, hands like hammers, the kind of build that made most men reconsider trouble before it started. But it wasn't just the size—it was the quiet. The way he sat, as if he belonged yet remained apart. Not a drifter. Not a miner. Someone who carried weight, even while sitting still.

He slid onto the stool beside him, signaling the bartender with a flick of his fingers. His voice, when it came, was casual, but measured. "Mind if I join you?"

The man took a slow sip, acknowledging the question with a glance before setting the glass down. "It's a free country." The words were careful, neutral, but beneath them lay an edge—a man accustomed to weighing intent.

He offered a slight nod, studying him as the bartender poured his drink. "You've got the look of a man who understands hard work." A pause, just long enough to let the thought settle. "This town's full of opportunities for those willing to take them."

A flicker of something passed across the man's face. Amusement? Skepticism? Hard to tell. He tilted his glass slightly. "Opportunities?" The word rolled slowly over his tongue. "Seems like those are reserved for the right kind of people."

He smiled, sharp and knowing. "Luck has its place. But a man makes his own fortune. Always has." He extended a hand. "William Donovan."

The man considered for a beat, then clasped it. His grip was firm, deliberate. "Samuel Hawkins."

He held his gaze a fraction longer than necessary.

"The way I see it, every man has his price and his breaking point. It's just about knowing which levers to pull." He leaned back, casual, his voice threaded with suggestion. "Butte's a chessboard, and I need men who can think beyond their next move."

Another drink, another moment to think, the whiskey burning clean down his throat. "And what's in it for me?" The question was quiet, measured. The beginning of something—or nothing at all.

A cigarette flared between William's fingers. "Partnership. Security. A chance to rise above the grind. I'm building something big. Could use a man with your talents."

He studied him, weighing the offer against whatever history sat behind his eyes. "Partnership and security are fine words, Donovan," he said finally. "But Butte's full of men with promises. What makes yours different?"

The answer came easily. "I see opportunities where others see obstacles. And I share the rewards with those who help me claim them." A pause, letting it settle. "You've been working the yards, breaking your back while the real money moves elsewhere. What if your strength became a stepping stone instead of a weight around your neck?"

He listened, suspicion lingering but interest piqued. The words carried the quiet lure of something more than survival. "And what exactly do you need from me?"

A test.

"A man who's not afraid to get his hands dirty. Someone to handle delicate matters. Someone who knows when to use his fists and when to keep them in his pockets. Someone who knows the value of silence. Someone I can trust."

The proposition hung between them, thick as the smoke curling toward the rafters. He weighed the moment, feeling the quiet gravity of the decision. "And if things go south? If this empire of yours doesn't hold?"

"Then we adapt. We overcome. And if we face adversity, you'll find I protect my own." Their eyes met, the weight of the moment shifting from proposition to something closer to agreement.

A long, slow nod. Samuel swirled the last of his whiskey before setting the glass down with finality. "Alright, Donovan. You've got yourself a partner. But let's be clear—loyalty's a two-way street."

"Agreed." A hand extended, met with another in a firm clasp. "Welcome aboard. Together, we're going to redefine power in Butte."

The deal was struck. Amid the clink of glasses and the quiet hum of ambition, a new alliance was forged— one built on strategy, necessity, and the quiet hunger for something greater.

In the din of the speakeasy, the moment passed unnoticed by most. But fate had been set into motion.

From a corner booth, another pair of eyes watched the exchange. He had seen these kinds of conversations before, the careful dance of proposition and acceptance. To any casual observer, it was just two men sharing drinks, but to him, it was something else entirely.

He waited until Samuel slipped into the crowd before making his move. Sliding into the recently vacated stool, he nodded toward the man across from him. "William Donovan, isn't it? I've heard you've got the Midas touch."

A slight hesitation, barely noticeable. "And you are?"

"James Morrison." He extended a hand, which William shook with careful appraisal. "Just a man trying to navigate this town."

"And what brings a man like you to a man like me?"

He leaned in slightly, lowering his voice. "I deal in information. And I have reason to believe that's a currency you value."

Interest flickered in his expression. "Go on."

"Butte's a complicated place. I understand its currents. Who moves where, who's pulling strings, where pressure points exist. I can offer insight—intelligence that could prove useful to a man with your ambitions."

A slow sip. A deliberate pause. "And in exchange?"

"A partnership. Security. A seat at the table."

The words settled between them, a chess move played with precision. William studied him, weighing possibilities. "And how do I know I can trust you? Loyalty is a rare commodity these days."

A smirk, quick and knowing. "Because, like you, I'm here to stake my claim. Our goals align. And in this town, it's wise to keep allies close—and potential partners even closer."

A long silence stretched between them before he reached for his drink. "You're playing a careful game, James."

"I intend to win it."

Another handshake. Another deal struck in the shadows of The Copper Vein. As the night swallowed them, both men knew that Butte wasn't just a town of opportunity—it was a battlefield. And only the most ruthless would walk away victorious.

The days in Butte were an amalgam of survival and observation, a delicate balance between making ends meet and absorbing the lifeblood of the town. Mornings meant work—any work that paid. Afternoons were spent walking the streets, ears tuned to the hum of shifting fortunes, eyes sharp for the undercurrents that ran deeper than the soot-streaked facades and raucous saloons.

The reporter had noticed him long before their paths officially crossed. From the vantage of his profession, he saw not just another drifter but a story waiting to be told. A man caught between movement and stillness, as if tethered to a past that refused to loosen its grip.

But it was the meeting outside the mining office that solidified his interest. The figure he'd been quietly watching had drawn the attention of someone else

—someone whose presence commanded more than casual curiosity.

The contrast between the two men was stark. The younger one, cautious, calculating, wearing the hardened expression of someone accustomed to slipping between the cracks. The other, William Donovan, a man who did not slip through cracks but carved his own path through them, cutting away what stood in his way.

Their conversation, though too distant to hear, unfolded in a silent rhythm of gestures. A nod, a measured tilt of the head. A pause, an interjection. One assessing, the other deliberating. The power dynamic was fluid—respect being tested, an unspoken negotiation at play.

The exchange left questions gnawing at him. What did a man like Donovan want with someone like that? And more importantly, what did the younger man have that made him worth the time?

He filed it away, a thread worth pulling.

The library, dim and quiet, carried the scent of aging paper and dust, a place where the noise of Butte softened into murmured inquiries and the occasional rustle of turning pages. He found him there, tucked between the shelves, lost in books meant for younger eyes but richer imaginations.

For nearly an hour, he watched from a distance. The way fingers traced illustrations, pausing with a reverence that spoke of longing rather than idle curiosity. The act of reading, or rather, seeing, carried a ritualistic quality—as if the images were less escape and more a tether to something unnamed.

It was this, more than anything, that made him approach.

He kept his tone light. "That one's got a way of pulling you in, doesn't it?"

A flicker of wariness. The book closed, not abruptly, but with an air of finality.

"James." A name given, clipped and spare.

He nodded, as if acknowledging an unspoken rule of exchange. "Ethan Bennett. I write for *The Butte Miner*." He gestured to the book still resting under the young man's fingertips. "You've got an eye for stories, I see."

A pause. A slow inhale, the weighing of words before offering them. "I like seeing places I've never been."

A simple answer. An answer meant to end the conversation.

He pressed gently. "I've seen you around. You've got a way of moving through this town like you're watching it unfold."

A flicker of something unreadable passed through the younger man's eyes. Suspicion. Curiosity. The tension between wanting to vanish and wanting to be known.

"I don't know what you're talking about." The

dismissal was there, but it lacked conviction.

Ethan leaned in slightly, lowering his voice just enough to shift the tone from casual to something more deliberate. "I've noticed you talking with Donovan."

That landed. The shift was immediate—shoulders squared, a breath drawn deeper than necessary. "You some kind of cop?"

He let out a quiet chuckle, shaking his head. "Nothing like that. Just a journalist trying to understand the town. And men like Donovan... they're part of its story."

A long silence stretched between them.

"I don't have a connection," came the eventual reply. "People talk. That's all."

He let the lie sit between them, unchallenged. Instead, he softened the angle. "Look, I'm not here to make trouble for you. I'm interested in the truth—the kind that doesn't make the headlines but runs beneath them. You see things, hear things. I think you could help me tell a story worth reading."

Another silence, but this one was different. Less defensive, more contemplative.

"I don't want any trouble."

"No trouble," he assured. "Just a story."

A breath. A nod. The smallest crack in the armor.

"Alright. But I'm not promising anything."

The corner of his mouth lifted in something resembling a smile. "That's all I ask."

As they parted, the agreement hung between them, fragile and unspoken. Trust, a rare currency in a town built on whispered deals and buried truths, had yet to be earned. But the first stone had been laid, and in a place like Butte, that was enough to start an empire— or bring one crashing down.

8

E than leveraged every contact he'd made through his reporting, digging into his network of whispers and favors. Determined to meet the man shaping Butte's undercurrent, his persistence paid off when a reliable source confirmed that William Donovan frequented *The Copper Vein* in the evenings. A place where business and pleasure mingled in the shadows, where allegiances were forged over poured whiskey and whispered deals.

Dressed to blend rather than stand out, he pushed through the heavy door that Thursday night, the low murmur of conversation and the clink of glasses setting the rhythm of the room. The scent of liquor, smoke, and ambition thickened the air.

In a shadowed corner, he held court, his presence an anchor amid the ebb and flow of the speakeasy. Beside him sat a solid wall of muscle—Samuel. The bruiser rarely spoke, but his mere existence was enough to quiet most tempers before they could flare. Their heads were bent together, words exchanged in a language of power.

At the bar, Ethan nursed a drink, heartbeat hammering against his ribs. He had waited for this moment, chased it through endless inquiries, and now, faced with it, the weight of it held him in place. He exhaled, drained the last of his whiskey, and slid from the stool.

The bruiser spotted him first. Muscle tensed, his body shifting—an instinctive barrier between him and the man he sought. It was a declaration in posture alone. A warning. Threats could wear any disguise, even that of a young reporter.

"Mr. Donovan." He extended a hand, a formal introduction despite the setting. "Ethan Bennett, *The Butte Miner.* I've—"

"I know who you are." The response was quick, edged with both amusement and intrigue. A subtle tilt of his head, a flicker of a smirk. "The Butte press must be getting ambitious."

Samuel eased back under Donovan's signal, though his watchful stance remained, eyes scanning for the first sign of trouble.

Ethan steadied himself. "I see Butte at a crossroads, and men like you are the architects of its future. I want to be part of that construction."

A flick of ash from a cigarette. The assessing gaze, the weight of silence. "Construction requires understanding the foundation, Mr. Bennett. Butte's foundation runs deep. More complex than most realize." A pause, a measured glance. "What makes you think you're ready to dig?"

Before he could answer, the atmosphere shifted. James slid into the seat beside the bruiser, a picture of casual confidence. He gestured for a cigarette, which was lit and passed without question. The grin he threw Ethan's way was equal parts amusement and challenge, a silent acknowledgment of the game afoot.

Ethan turned back to Donovan. "I'm not afraid of getting my hands dirty. I've got skills. Insight. I can be useful."

A chuckle—low, knowing. "Insight is always in short supply. But insight without action is like a miner without a pick. Useless."

Samuel finally spoke, voice deliberate. "And action can be costly. You prepared for that, Bennett?"

A new voice cut through the tension. "He seems prepared enough. Tracked down the elusive William Donovan, after all." James smirked as he exhaled smoke. "That's more than most can say."

Ethan seized the moment. "Exactly. I'm not just another journalist looking for a story—I see the bigger picture. I can contribute."

"Vision is one thing." Donovan leaned forward, fingers tapping against the table. "Seeing it through is another. This town stands at a crossroads. Its path depends as much on will as it does on vision. Why come to me?"

"I'm a journalist, yes. But my ambitions go beyond the printed page. I see Butte transforming, and I don't want to be an observer. I want in."

The simplicity of it cut through the air. No embellishment. No disguise. Samuel stiffened at the audacity, muscles flexing beneath his coat. Donovan, unreadable, studied him through the dim haze of the speakeasy.

"You want in." The words hung there, measured, weighed. Donovan leaned back slightly, a finger idly tapping against his glass. "We're not running a social club, Bennett. The stakes are high, the game played far from the public eye."

He let the silence stretch just long enough to make him question if he'd overplayed his hand. Then, almost lazily, he flicked a glance at Samuel—an unspoken exchange passing between them.

"A journalist," he murmured at last, as if turning the word over in his mind, testing its weight. His lips twitched, not quite a smile. "Now, that's interesting."

He nodded, unwavering. "I understand the risks."

"Loyalty is a word easily spoken, Mr. Bennett, but

harder to live by. Especially here." His voice dipped lower. "You're proposing a dangerous game—for yourself, and for us."

"I know," his voice steady. "And I want in anyway."

A pause. Long enough to stretch, to test.

"If you're serious," Donovan finally said, "you'll have to prove yourself."

The door cracked open—not fully, not freely, but enough to let him step through. Enough to offer a glimpse of the world he had fought to reach. Not acceptance, not yet. But a beginning.

As he left *The Copper Vein* that night, the weight of his choice settled on his shoulders, equal parts exhilaration and unease. The four of them—each bound by their own hunger—were now moving toward a singular path. Power, control, and the sharp edges of ambition.

But in Butte, fortunes were made on the blade of cunning. And just as quickly lost to those who faltered.

He had taken his first step into the dark. Whether he would rise or be swallowed whole was yet to be seen.

9

The strike had gutted Butte, leaving its streets thick with tension, its air charged with defiance. Marking a pivotal moment in the town's storied history with the Anaconda Copper Mining Company at its epicenter. From the moment picketers locked arms across Anaconda Road, the town became a battlefield, the silence of stalled industry speaking louder than the drills that once tore through rock.

By the second day, the miners had succeeded. The city's lifeblood—copper—remained trapped beneath the earth, waiting for hands that refused to work.

Then the paper hit.

The 'Butte Daily Bulletin' printed what had been whispered in bunkhouses and backrooms: that men at the top of the Anaconda Copper Mining Company had spoken of dealing with the strike through bullets and nooses. Maybe it was true. Maybe it wasn't. But in the saloons where loyalty was measured in broken knuckles, and in the kitchens where wives counted the coins left from last week's pay, belief had always been more dangerous than fact.

In August, the situation reached a boiling point outside the Neversweat Mine, one of Anaconda's key operations. A few hundred held the line outside the Neversweat Mine, their voices raised, their backs stiff with resolve. The reasons remain murky, lost in the chaos that followed, but the outcome was tragically clear. Anaconda mine guards opened fire on the unarmed picketers, unleashing a hail of bullets. Sixteen hit the dirt. One never got back up. Tom Manning, unarmed, shot in the back as he ran.

The aftermath of the shooting saw the arrival of federal troops a day later, a move officially intended to prevent further bloodshed. Yet, the presence of military boots on the ground only served to underscore the severity of the conflict that had taken hold of Butte.

Amidst this turmoil, voices of dissent were systematically silenced. A labor newspaper, which had dared to speak out about the strike and its violent suppression, found itself suppressed, its right to free expression curtailed by forces aligned with the interests of Anaconda.

Three weeks later, the strike collapsed under hunger

and exhaustion. The mines reopened. The men who had fought for dignity walked back into the tunnels, the weight of their defeat pressing heavier than the rock above their heads. As for Manning, there was an inquest, the kind designed to silence rather than seek truth. Anaconda's men took the stand, their stories neat and uniform, polished to match the company line. The boarding house workers, those who had seen the guards raise their rifles, spoke just as plainly—but their words carried no weight.

In the end, the verdict was handed down. *Killed by a bullet fired by persons unknown.*

Anaconda remained untouchable.

His death, and the events that led to it, remain a dark chapter in Butte's history, a reminder of the struggles that have shaped the town and its people.

In the tense aftermath of the miners' strike, with the town still simmering from the recent violence and the arrival of federal troops, the delicate balance of power and public perception teetered on the edge of a knife. It was during this charged atmosphere that William Donovan saw an opportunity to solidify his influence and test the loyalty of his newest associate, Ethan Bennett.

In the days that followed, *The Copper Vein* became more than a speakeasy. It was a war room. A summons came, pulling him from the newsroom's ink-stained clutter into the low-lit hush of a backroom where power spoke in murmurs. The air was thick—whiskey, cigar smoke, and something else, something heavier.

He stepped inside.

At the head of the table sat William, the one who had called him here, unreadable as ever. To his right, Samuel, arms folded, eyes watchful. Across from him, James, cigarette poised between two fingers, his smile thin, considering.

"Ethan," he began, his voice low and steady, "you've told me you're ready to do whatever it takes. Today, you're going to prove that." Acutely aware of the significance of the moment, he nodded. "I'm ready. What do you need me to do?"

He slid a piece of paper across the table towards him. A rewrite of the truth. The miners painted as agitators, outsiders. The bloodshed at the Neversweat Mine reframed as self-defense. Anaconda's men cast as victims of a lawless mob.

He picked up the paper, his eyes scanning the contents —a prepared statement, rife with falsehoods designed to shift public perception, painting the striking miners as agitators and outsiders, underplaying the violence, and praising the restraint of the Anaconda mine guards.

"You'll print this in *The Butte Miner*," he continued, "Public sentiment is slipping in the wrong direction. Time to remind them where their loyalties lie."

His fingers curled around the edge of the paper. The ink bled certainty where there was none.

"And if I don't?"

A slow smile. "Then you're of no use to me. And in Butte, a man with no use is a man with no future."

His heart sank as he absorbed the implications of William's request. To print such lies would compromise every journalistic principle he held dear. Yet, refusal would mean breaking his pledge to him and potentially endangering his position and future here.

Samuel at his side didn't move, but the silence spoke for him. James, still lounging, exhaled smoke and flicked away spent ash, watching, waiting.

The weight of the moment settled.

For years, he had chased stories, stripped lies from the bodies of men who wore them like second skins. He knew the power of words. He had seen them ignite revolutions. He had seen them bury bodies.

This wasn't truth. This was a weapon.

Manning's name flickered in his mind, swallowed by silence, buried under the weight of men who had sworn the guards never fired.

Then, another thought. Not of justice, not of principle. But of power. Of why he had come to Butte. What he had wanted when he first set foot on its streets.

Power wasn't in truth. It was a blade sharpened in ink, a weapon aimed at the city's conscience.

A breath.

He set the paper down. The glass was already refilled. The ink had already begun to dry.

10

The whiskey tasted different after he chose a side. Thicker. Heavier. The kind of weight a man only feels when he stops asking questions —and starts knowing the answers. Suspicion, once the quiet undercurrent between them, gave way to something sharper—an unspoken understanding forged in the shadows of Butte's treacherous streets. Nights at 'The Copper Vein' stretched long, whiskey poured in steady hands, cigarette smoke curling through the air as ambition laid itself bare between them.

He became more than a guide—he was an architect of understanding, mapping out the town's hidden corridors, the backroom dealings, the silent handshakes that determined a man's fate before he even stepped into daylight. Butte had its own laws, and he was learning them in whiskey-glazed conversations, folded in the dim corners of the speakeasy where men spoke not in truths, but in careful omissions.

Ethan, once an observer, had become something else. He dressed sharper, carried himself with the self-assurance of a man who belonged. His articles, once filled with questions, now held answers—crafted ones, tailored to fit William's needs. His colleagues at 'The Butte Miner' watched, murmuring. He felt their eyes on him when he entered the office, but he didn't flinch. He was part of something bigger now. He wasn't just writing history—he was making it.

But power had a cost.

A lull had settled over the place, the din of laughter thinning as the night stretched on. Glasses clinked, voices dipped low. He leaned back, swirling amber liquid in his glass, watching the way it caught the light. Across from him, James exhaled smoke, the embers at his fingertips flickering between the moments of their conversation.

"You ever think about the cost?" The words slipped out before he could stop them. A quiet admission. A question meant less for an answer than for the space it occupied between them.

He didn't meet his gaze right away. He studied the last of his drink, the weight of the question settling between them like dust before a storm. "Every day." A slow inhale. "But here, cost is just part of the game. You don't play, you don't win. You just watch someone else take what could've been yours."

Samuel grunted, shifting slightly, the movement slow, deliberate. "The stakes are high, but the rewards are higher. We're in Donovan's corner now. That means we play by his rules. And Donovan doesn't pay for his own liquor."

His grip tightened around his glass. "Yeah. But at what point does the cost outweigh the reward? We've seen what happens to men who fall out of favor. Where do we draw the line?"

James leaned in, his expression unreadable in the low light. "We draw the line where it keeps us breathing, Ethan. We stay useful. We stay sharp. That's how we climb. And we don't look down."

Samuel nodded, striking a match against the table's edge, the flare of flame catching in his eyes. "Loyalty's the only thing keeping our heads above ground. You start drawing lines, you start wondering what side of 'em you stand on."

He studied them both, their conviction worn like armor. He felt it pressing in on him—the weight of something shifting beneath his skin. You ever think we're just circling the drain here? The thought sat heavy on his tongue, but he didn't voice it. Instead, he drained the last of his drink and forced a smirk.

"Maybe we're not just climbing. Maybe we're building something worth standing on."

James lifted his glass in a silent toast, the moment lingering, a fragile truce between doubt and ambition.

Then the door swung open.

A group of miners stepped inside, their presence cutting through the warmth of the speakeasy like a blade. Their movements slow, deliberate. Faces hardened, shadows of the strike still etched into the lines of their skin.

He felt it before it happened. The shift in the air, the hush that followed, the weight of eyes settling on him. A moment stretched too thin.

One of the miners—broad-shouldered, the scar of a burn curling along his jaw—took a step closer, his breath thick with whiskey and exhaustion. "You're the pen behind the lies, ain't ya?"

Silence splintered. The room, once filled with the casual hum of conversation, had gone still. Even the bartender hesitated, hand hovering near the glass he had been polishing.

Another voice. "The voice of Donovan's cronies, telling us we're the villains in our own fight."

He felt his own pulse hammering at the base of his throat. This is what it means to pick a side.

Samuel's chair scraped against the floor, a slow, deliberate sound. He didn't move much—he didn't have to. Just straightened, broad shoulders squared. "Do you have a problem?"

Not a question. A warning.

The miners bristled, anger simmering just beneath their skin. "The problem," one spat, "is you lot, cozying up with Donovan, spreading lies about us. You think you can just write us off?"

James leaned back, rolling his cigarette between his fingers, watching the tension coil. "Maybe you should learn to read between the lines."

The air snapped taut. The bartender stopped polishing. A chair shifted somewhere in the back, someone moving to get a better look.

"Look, it was a job," he started, but the words felt wrong in his mouth. Too light for what they carried. The miners weren't buying it—hell, neither was he.

Laughter. Bitter, sharp. "A job? Selling your soul, more like."

One of the miners took a step closer. Scarred hands clenched into fists.

Samuel tilted his head, voice dropping to something dark, quiet. "We can settle this outside."

The miner hesitated. A choice lingered between them, teetering on the edge of a breath. The room held its stance, waiting for the first move.

James smirked, about to speak—then hesitated. Just for a second. His gaze flicked to the miners' hands, but there was something else in his eyes. A calculation. A thought he swallowed down before it could surface. Then, just as fast, the grin returned, and the cigarette flicked away. "Forget these clowns. They're not worth the dirt on your boots."

The words cut deep, but they were enough. The moment broke. The miners hesitated, weighing fury against consequence. And then, like a storm losing its fury, they turned away, retreating to a corner table, voices lowered, anger still simmering beneath their skin.

Ethan let out a slow breath, only now realizing his fingers had curled into fists.

Samuel took a drag from his cigarette, exhaled smoke like it carried the last of his patience. "Next time, don't try to explain. Just let them know where you stand."

James laughed, slapping him on the back. "Welcome to the real Butte."

The miners had backed down, but their stares lingered, pressing against his skin like a blade held just short of flesh. The night carried on, laughter returning in cautious waves, but something had changed. Ethan sat, staring at the last drops of whiskey in his glass, and for the first time, he wasn't sure whose words he was drinking down—his own, or Donovan's.

Words weren't just ink on paper anymore.

They had consequences.

And the next time, the cost might not be so easily walked away from.

The night stretched on, but something lingered in the air long after the confrontation faded. A warning. A promise. A question, left unspoken.

The bar returned to laughter. But Ethan swore he still heard the echoes of something breaking. He didn't know it yet, but something else was waiting to break before the night was through.

11

The bar had emptied, but Samuel's rage lingered, coiled tight in his shoulders. "Tonight's going to get busy," he murmured to Ethan and James, his voice low and flint-hard. Not a suggestion. A sentence passed.

They waited. Watched. Until the miners staggered out into the night, their boots scraping the quiet street. The door of The Copper Vein swung shut behind them, and in its hush, something shifted. The signal had been given.

The fight ignited a block or so from the bar, beneath the brittle eye of the moon. The air was cold, brittle, sharpened by tension. No words were exchanged as the three of them emerged from the shadows. None were needed.

One of the miners turned, breath steaming. His laugh was hollow. "What now? You lads looking for an autograph?"

Samuel stepped forward, calm and dangerous. "No. Just thought you could use a reminder. About who runs this town."

The miner squared up, jaw jutting. "Is that so? You and what army, pretty boy?"

For a moment, Ethan wondered if there might be a way to walk past. To speak instead. But that moment passed like smoke in the wind.

The first hit cracked the silence. Samuel's fist found the man's jaw, clean and fast. The sound echoed off brick, sharp as gunfire.

What followed was not chaos—it was choreography. A brutal dance. Fists. Elbows. The thud of bone on flesh. The wet snap of cartilage giving way.

Ethan moved without thought. No pen. No page. Just flesh, fear, and the hot thrill of purpose. The weight of a life turning. The strike of his knuckles a punctuation mark. Not a question—a statement.

He'd never fought like this before. Not with this kind of clarity. Every movement was a rejection of the man he used to be. The ink-stained kid with a suitcase full of notebooks. That man was gone, left behind in the alley with every blow.

He belonged now. Not to ideals. But to something harder. Meaner. Real.

Samuel fought with precision, economy. No wasted

motion. No mercy. He was a machine with a cause. Watching him out of the corner of his eye, he registered the change—a flash of something grim and useful. A man re-forging himself in violence.

James fought differently. Not with discipline, but with desperation. Wild, feral energy. He saw the miner in front of him, but he saw others, too. Ghosts. His father's silhouette. That basement door. That smell. The fists came hard, fast, filled with years of silence and rage. He didn't speak. He roared.

The miners tried. They fought back, swinging heavy and scared. But they were tired, half-drunk, scattered. The trio fought with unity, with purpose, with something to prove.

When it ended, it ended fast. The miners scattered, limping into the shadows, bloodied and broken. No victory was declared. None needed to be. It was written on the sidewalk in spit and blood.

They stood together, catching breath. He wiped his mouth, tasted iron. James leaned against the wall, chest heaving. Samuel lit a cigarette with steady hands, the flare of the match painting his face in red.

No one spoke. But something had shifted.

For him, it was more than a fight. It was an initiation. He wasn't observing anymore. He was inside the story now, part of its machinery. He'd crossed a line and hadn't looked back.

For James, it was release. A kind of cleansing. Not of pain, but of silence. Every blow a word he'd never said. Every bruise a line of the truth he'd hidden.

And for Samuel, it was confirmation. This was the crew. These were the men worth betting on. Men who didn't blink. Men who understood that power wasn't handed over—it was taken, tooth by tooth.

They walked back slowly, their shadows long behind them. No cheers. No glory. Just the sound of their steps echoing off cold stone. They had proven something tonight. To each other. To the streets. To themselves.

Belonging had a price. They had paid it in full.

12

As Butte's mining operations clattered on, the town trembled with a new kind of tension —not the rumble of drills or the cries from shafts, but a quieter, more insidious hum. A contested mining claim. A whisper in the smoke-thick saloons. A name: Josephine Storar.

She had inherited her father's land, his veins of copper, and the weight of a legacy carved into the stone of the earth. But amid the ledgers and lode maps, one line had been missed—a valuable tract, assumed hers, was never properly registered. In the eyes of the law, it was a shadow. And shadows, in Butte, were dangerous things.

William Donovan, whose empire grew not in inches but in intentions, caught wind of the oversight through Ethan. The claim bordered his own holdings, a jagged puzzle piece that, if acquired, would give him dominion over the richest seam this side of the Rockies.

"Josephine Storar is preparing for a fight," Ethan said in the back room of The Copper Vein, the smoke curling like script above their heads. "The claim's heading to court, but it's already chaos. Everyone with a pickaxe or a pocketbook wants a slice."

William leaned back, his fingers steepled, eyes narrowing. "She won't fold. Not easily. But the courts, the papers, the noise—that can be shaped. And a spectacle, Ethan, is just a stage for men like us."

Josephine had her father's blood and none of his naivety. She saw the storm coming. Refused to blink. At a gathering of miners in a half-collapsed union hall, her voice rang out: "My father built this with his hands. This claim is his legacy, and I'll defend it—in court or out."

Her conviction rippled through the crowd. Butte had always respected defiance, even in women.

Back in Donovan's circle, things began to move. James leaned into the strategy, eyes gleaming with the promise of conflict. "Legalities be damned," he said, flicking ash into the void. "Butte's never run on paper. It's pick and power that decides things. She wants to drag it through court? Fine. But we don't wait on verdicts. We act."

Ethan watched him. Something in him had hardened. The courtroom was no longer a path to justice, only an obstacle to be stepped over. Samuel, silent and coiled, gave a single nod. "If it turns physical, we're ready."

Ethan felt the adrenaline spark low in his chest. This was no longer about facts or fairness. It was about force. And force, when used cleverly, carved out empires.

"We do this smart," he said, steadying himself. "Pressure the right people. Watch for cracks. She has allies—cut them off. She has pride—use it. We don't need to crush her. We just need her to stumble."

James grinned. "That's the spirit."

The three of them—the blade, the hammer, and the pen—set their plan in motion. Strategy drafted not in ink, but in implication. In leverage. In fear.

The courtroom day approached, and Butte braced. The Storar claim had become more than a patch of land. It was a symbol—of legacy, of power, of who this town would belong to when the smoke cleared.

And in the streets, where names were made and buried in the same breath, the question echoed louder than the drills ever had: who would walk away owning the dirt, and who would be buried beneath it?

13

The courthouse loomed beneath a slate-grey sky, its stone façade a monument to justice —or the illusion of it. Inside, the murmur of voices held a tautness, as if the walls themselves anticipated what was to come. The disputed claim, nestled between two of Donovan's most productive shafts, promised not just ore—but dominion. It had gathered momentum, dragging in miners, speculators, and powerbrokers alike. Today, Butte would bear witness.

Josephine Storar sat composed at the petitioner's table. Her dark coat was modest, but the way she carried herself filled the room with presence. She was not her father, but she carried his fire—the same defiance that had once carved tunnels into these hills. At her side stood Phinnaeus Brandon, her attorney brought in from New York, the cut of his suit as sharp as his rhetoric.

Across the aisle, William Donovan occupied his place with the studied ease of a man who had never been denied. Ethan and James flanked him, their silence a kind of armor. Samuel stood apart, arms crossed at the back of the room, like a storm *on pause.*

The Honorable Judge Douglas Reid raised his gavel and brought the room to a hush. The oak-paneled courtroom, with its high ceilings and brass chandeliers, seemed to lean forward, listening.

"This court is now in session," he intoned, his voice a steady echo in the stillness. "We are here to resolve the matter of the disputed mining claim between *Storar Mining & Milling Company*, represented by Ms. Josephine Storar, and *Donovan Consolidated Mining*, represented by Mr. William Donovan. Mr. Brandon, your opening statement, please."

At the petitioner's table, Josephine Storar sat with quiet authority, the name of her family's company etched into the minds of most in Butte. *Storar Mining & Milling* was more than a business—it was a monument to perseverance. Her father's initials were still visible on the cast-iron sign over the mine entrance, blackened by time and soot. This fight wasn't just about land. It was about memory.

She gave a subtle nod to her counsel, and Phinnaeus Brandon rose. The cut of his suit whispered Manhattan, but his gaze was steel. "Ladies and gentlemen of the court," he began, folding his hands over the lectern, "today, we stand not just to defend a mining claim, but a legacy. *Storar Mining & Milling Company* has operated in good faith on the contested parcel since 1910, when Mr. John Storar—pioneer, builder, and citizen—first pulled copper from those hills."

He paused, letting silence punctuate the lineage.

"Now, due to a bureaucratic oversight—an unsigned registration slip, lost in the shuffling of war-era files—*Donovan Consolidated Mining* would have you believe that this land is unclaimed. That history can be unmade with ink and omission."

Across the room, William Donovan sat impassive, a hint of amusement curling at the corner of his mouth. Beside him, Ethan and James watched in stillness. Donovan's empire had grown quickly—*Donovan Consolidated* was known for swallowing claims like a rising tide. Ambition in a tailored suit.

Brandon continued, laying documents on the evidence table with the precision of a man slicing through noise. "Here are tax receipts. Maintenance logs. Payrolls. Decades of activity—proof that the Storar family never once abandoned their claim."

The courtroom was silent, the audience hanging on Brandon's every word as he skillfully navigated the nuances of mining law, interspersing legal arguments with anecdotes of the Storar family's contributions to Butte's community.

"And this," he said, lifting a faded deed, "is the original map. Signed by the hand of John Storar himself. It predates *Donovan Consolidated Mining's* interest by half a century."

He turned now to Judge Reid, voice sharpened to a scalpel's edge.

"As for the so-called dispute," Brandon said, his tone sharpening, "it is nothing more than an attempt to capitalize on a technical oversight for personal gain. It disregards the principles of fairness, equity, and respect for those who have built their lives around these mines."

Turning to address the judge directly, Brandon concluded, "Your Honor, this case is about more than just a piece of land. It's about honoring the legacy of those who came before us and protecting the rights of those who dare to dream of a better future for Butte. We ask that you recognize the validity of the original claim registration, despite its clerical imperfections, and affirm *Storar Mining & Milling Company's* rightful ownership."

As Brandon took his seat, a murmur of approval rippled through the courtroom, his compelling presentation leaving an indelible mark on the proceedings.

The Judge nodded thoughtfully, his expression unreadable. Across the room, William exchanged a glance with his lawyer, a silent acknowledgment of the formidable case they were up against. Brandon's opening salvo had set a high bar for him to meet.

Donovan's attorney rose next. A competent man with the polish of a company man and the spine of a ledger. "Your Honor," he began, "while we respect the history Mr. Brandon has so eloquently presented, the law must concern itself not with sentiment, but with statutes. The issue at hand is not one of legacy, but of legality. *Donovan Consolidated Mining's* interest in the disputed claim is supported by the principles of the Apex Law, which clearly states the rights of miners to follow a vein, even if it extends beneath land owned by another. The Apex Law exists for a reason—and *Donovan Consolidated Mining* has abided by its every letter. "

The lawyer then cleverly tried to pivot the argument towards the benefits of the Apex Law for Butte's broader mining community, subtly suggesting that *Donovan Consolidated's* acquisition of the claim could serve the greater good. "The Apex Law was designed to ensure the efficient and productive use of our mineral resources. *Donovan Consolidated Mining's* actions are not only within his legal rights but also in the best interest of Butte's economic future.

Under the stern gaze of Judge Reid, the legal battle over the disputed mining claim unfolded with increasing intensity. Phinnaeus Brandon stood poised, his voice resonating with conviction as he prepared to counter the arguments presented by

Donovan Consolidated's counsel.

"Your Honor," he began, "I must object to my learned colleague's interpretation of the Apex Law in this context. The law, while indeed designed to facilitate mining, was never intended to disenfranchise landowners based on technicalities or oversight."

Judge Reid, known for his no-nonsense approach, leaned forward, his expression one of focused attention. "Mr. Brandon, please elucidate your objections for the court. Be specific."

Seizing the opportunity, he responded, "Certainly, Your Honor. The Apex Law allows miners to follow a vein or lode of ore across property lines vertically. However, the claim in dispute here does not involve a vein that extends into property owned by *Donovan Consolidated Mining*. Instead, we are dealing with a surface claim, clearly demarcated and worked upon by the *Storar Mining & Milling Company* for decades."

He continued, "To apply the Apex Law in this instance would set a dangerous precedent, effectively allowing any miner to lay claim to land on the merest pretense of subterranean continuity. This is not the spirit of the law, nor is it just."

Donovan's lawyer, undeterred, rose to reply. "Your Honor, while we appreciate Mr. Brandon's concerns, it is our position that the disputed claim falls squarely within the purview of the Apex Law. The documentation we have submitted clearly shows—"

"Documentation that is, at best, ambiguous," Brandon interjected, his tone sharpening. "And at worst, a deliberate attempt to misinterpret the law for personal gain."

Judge Reid raised a hand, signaling for silence. "Gentlemen, let's maintain decorum. Mr. Brandon, you've made your point. Please proceed."

He nodded, turning his attention back to the judge. "Thank you, Your Honor. It is our contention that *Storar Mining & Milling Company's* claim, though lacking in the precise bureaucratic formalities, has been recognized and respected by this community and this industry for over a generation. To upend that understanding now, on the basis of a questionable legal maneuver, would not only harm the Storar family but could destabilize the very foundation of property rights in Butte."

The judge, his expression thoughtful, turned to *Donovan Consolidated's* lawyer. "And what of the claims of other parties involved? This court is aware that there are more interests here than just those of *Donovan Consolidated Mining* and *Storar Mining & Milling Company.*"

Donovan's lawyer acknowledged the point. "Yes, Your Honor. While there are indeed multiple claims, it is our belief that a ruling in favor of *Donovan Consolidated Mining* would allow for a consolidation of these claims, leading to more efficient and productive mining operations."

Judge Reid leaned back, the weight of the decision before him clear in his furrowed brow. "This court recognizes the complexities of this case and the passions it has inflamed. The Apex Law, property rights, the legacy of the Storar family, and the future of mining in Butte—all are at stake."

He paused, letting his words hang in the air. "I will take all arguments under advisement. This court will reconvene tomorrow morning for my ruling. Until then, I urge all parties to consider not just the letter of the law, but the spirit of this community and the legacy we wish to leave for future generations."

The gavel fell.

As the courtroom emptied, the tension remained, a palpable entity that followed each participant out into the street. The day's proceedings had laid bare the intricacies of law, the depth of personal conviction, and the enduring struggle over the land that defined them all.

Outside, the wind had picked up. Ethan and James lingered on the steps, watching Josephine descend with her lawyer.

"She's tougher than she looks," James said, lighting a cigarette. "Would've made a hell of a politician." Ethan said nothing. He watched her vanish into the crowd and felt a strange disquiet settle in his chest.

This wasn't just about power anymore.

It was about the story they were writing in stone, with blood, with silence.

And tomorrow, one sentence—one ruling—might change everything.

14

William, ensconced in the dusky solitude of his study, watched the fire flicker in the hearth, each flame a whisper of uncertainty. The courtroom showdown had played out with the gravity he anticipated, yet as the evening deepened, unease clung to him like coal dust. For all his calculated moves in the mines and saloons of Butte, this particular gamble bore stakes that gnawed deeper than any before.

Earlier that night, he'd acted with uncharacteristic desperation. A bribe—one hundred thousand dollars—placed in an envelope and dispatched like a flare into darkness. Not offered lightly, but issued with the full knowledge that the disputed claim was no ordinary patch of dirt. It was the keystone in his growing empire, the final thread in a tapestry woven from ambition and blood.

James and Ethan had been dispatched under the cloak of night, their footsteps muffled on the leaf-strewn walkway leading to the home of the Honorable Judge Douglas Reid. Their mission was clear, though the weight of it settled like lead in their chests. This was no longer maneuvering. It was a proposition to bend justice itself.

James moved with the precision of habit, his expression unreadable, while Ethan, a beat behind, felt the sting of conscience with each step. He clutched the envelope, its contents humming with implication.

James rapped firmly on the door, the knock echoing like a challenge in the quiet.

Judge Reid answered, stern-faced beneath the porch light.

"Judge Reid, good evening, Sir." He began, his voice smooth, practiced. "We are here on behalf of Mr. Donovan. He believes it to be in the best interest of Butte for the disputed claim to be resolved swiftly... and favorably."

Behind him, Ethan extended the envelope—a gesture heavy with implication.

Judge Reid's gaze narrowed. "And Mr. Donovan believes that my decision can be bought with an envelope full of cash? You tell Mr. Donovan that my integrity is not for sale."

He did not flinch. "Your Honor, it's a pragmatic solution to a complex problem. It's not just about the claim—it's about Butte's future. This... gesture is merely a token of Mr. Donovan's commitment to that future."

The judge stepped forward, casting a long shadow. "Mr. Morrison, Mr. Bennett, I've spent my career upholding the law, ensuring justice is served without prejudice. What you're suggesting insults not only my position but the very fabric of this community. I would advise you both to reconsider your current path before it's too late."

Ethan shifted. His words had carved something open inside him, exposing the soft, unspoken question: when had they stopped believing in lines that couldn't be crossed?

James, slower now, nodded once. "Your Honor, we meant no disrespect. We'll convey your message to Mr. Donovan."

They turned, the envelope unopened between them, a paper-thin promise of ruin. Behind them, the judge's voice followed, low and weighty.

"Gentlemen, Butte stands at a crossroads. The decisions we make today will echo through its future. Choose wisely."

The walk back to Donovan's home was soundless, save for the crunch of gravel beneath their shoes. Each step pressed their choices deeper into the dirt.

At his desk, William turned a glass of whiskey in his hand. The amber caught in the lamplight, casting fractured reflections across the polished surface. He sipped, but it did little to loosen the grip of something coiled in his chest, slow as smoke and just as suffocating. He'd played a high card. And now he waited to see who would call the bluff.

But he did not hedge his bets on one front alone. As they returned empty-handed, he dispatched Samuel to Josephine Storar's doorstep. Where coin failed, shadow might prevail.

The porch was quiet, the air cut with winter's edge. Samuel stood in the halo of the porch light, a silhouette shaped by menace and resolve.

"Ms. Storar," he said, voice smooth, cold. "We find ourselves at a crossroads, you and I. Mr. Donovan has a vision for this town—a vision that doesn't include protracted disputes over claims."

Josephine appeared in the doorway, posture unbending. "Your vision," she said, eyes fierce, "seems to be clouded by greed. You may think to intimidate me into submission, but I assure you, Mr. Hawkins, I am no wilting flower to be trampled underfoot."

The moon's shadows cut deep into his features. "It's not intimidation, Ms. Storar. It's reality. The ground's shifting beneath your feet, Ms. Storar. Those who don't move get buried."

Her laughter was short, sharp. "Your brand of lawlessness? You mistake my determination for weakness. I was raised on granite, Mr. Hawkins. You'll need more than wind and bluster to break me."

He stepped closer. "This isn't just about weathering storms, Ms. Storar. It's about surviving them. Mr. Donovan doesn't lose, and he's not about to start with you."

"Surviving?" Her words were steel. "I've done more than survive, Mr. Hawkins. I've thrived, and I will continue to do so, with or without Mr. Donovan's approval. This land is my birthright, and I will defend it with every resource at my disposal."

He held her gaze, but the threat had met its match.

"You're playing a dangerous game, Ms. Storar," he warned, voice lowered. "Mr. Donovan has resources you can't begin to comprehend. It would be a... shame for things to become unpleasant."

She stepped into the light, defiant. "And you can relay to Mr. Donovan that I have resources of my own. Resources that are not to be underestimated. Butte is more than its mines; it's its people. And we protect our own."

The message was delivered. The threat received.

"This isn't over, Ms. Storar," he said, turning.

Her voice followed him. "I'll be waiting."

As he disappeared into the shadows, the porch remained lit, her figure still, unyielding. The encounter had been a battle of wills, one neither would forget.

Night draped the town in silence. William stood at the window, a silhouette against his own uncertainty. The silhouettes of mining rigs loomed in the distance, silent sentinels to his ambitions. This courtroom drama laced with principles and defiance—was different. He had risen through grit and shadows, but this—this was daylight reckoning.

The ticking clock filled the room with its steady reminder: morning would come, and with it, a ruling.

The bribe. The veiled threats. Each was a string in the fragile web he had spun. And now, with dawn creeping across the slag heaps, all he could do was wait—listening for the tremor that would signal the cave-in.

15

The courtroom was hushed, solemn as a church before the sermon. The air hung dense, thick with expectation. Even the sunlight filtering through the high windows seemed reluctant to disturb the stillness. At the bench, the Honorable Judge Douglas Reid adjusted his glasses and looked out over the gathered crowd with the gravity of a man about to cast ripples through the bedrock of Butte.

"Having reviewed the arguments presented by both parties," he began, his voice a metronome of control, "this court finds in favor of the Storar Mining & Milling Company."

A ripple passed through the room—half gasp, half exhale. Relief, outrage, disbelief—all spilled into the charged air.

Josephine Storar stood tall beside Phinnaeus Brandon, the flare of victory rising behind her eyes like dawn through smoke. The room saw a woman vindicated, but what stirred beneath her quiet smile was something stronger than satisfaction—it was the steel of a legacy reclaimed. For her, this was never about a plot of land. It was about lineage, principle, and survival. And she had stood unbent.

Across the aisle, William did not move. He sat as still as stone, unreadable, while Ethan and James exchanged glances, the weight of the verdict settling in their chests. Donovan Consolidated Mining had lost a keystone. And everyone in that room knew the implications.

Judge Reid's gavel struck once, calling the court back to stillness. "Before we conclude," he said, his voice deepening, his gaze now fixed on William Donovan, "this court must address a grave matter brought to light during these proceedings."

Tension returned, thicker now, drawn tight across the room.

"It has come to my attention that there were attempts to improperly influence the outcome of this case —including acts of intimidation, and an audacious attempt to bribe a public official. Myself."

A collective inhale, sharp as a whistle through a mine shaft.

"Such actions undermine the very foundation of justice," the judge said, every syllable weighty. "This court—and this town—will not be held hostage by the ambitions of powerful men."

His gaze never left Donovan. "Mr. Donovan, consider this a formal warning. Should you, or anyone under your direction, attempt to subvert justice again, the law will respond without mercy."

Donovan did not flinch. His posture remained unchanged, but inside, gears shifted. The public rebuke was more than a blow—it was a fracture in his carefully maintained armor. And as Reid's words echoed, Donovan's mind was already rebuilding, recalibrating. His empire had absorbed blows before. This one would be no different.

As the gavel fell, signaling adjournment, Donovan stood slowly, his movements deliberate. Around him, the low murmur of the crowd began to swell—speculation, judgment, awe. The corridors of power were shifting, and everyone could feel it.

Outside, under a sky scraped clean by wind, the confrontation found new footing.

"Ms. Storar," Donovan said, his tone low, intimate in its menace. "You may think this little legal victory changes something. It doesn't. Butte respects power. And I have more of it than you can imagine."

Josephine turned to face him fully, her chin high, her voice unflinching. "Mr. Donovan, I was raised on this land. I've buried men braver than you and built with less. Your threats mean nothing. Respect doesn't come from fear—it comes from standing your ground. And

I've done just that."

He stepped closer, but she held firm.

"Be careful, Ms. Storar. There are more ways to lose a claim than through the courts."

"And there are more ways to win than you'll ever understand," she replied. "You've underestimated me once. Don't do it again."

Her words were not merely defiant—they were a vow. And Donovan heard it.

Ethan stood near the courthouse steps, watching them. Something in her stance struck him. Not her courage—he had seen that. It was her clarity. The same clarity he'd begun to lose.

James beside him, arms crossed, jaw tight.

"She's not backing down," he muttered. It wasn't admiration in his voice. It was recognition. The same heat he carried inside, the same stubborn fire.

Ethan said nothing. In her defiance, he saw what had once lived in him—before the lines had blurred, before the envelopes, before the silence. Her fight, uncorrupted, struck something raw. For the first time, he wondered if they were on the wrong side of a story that would be told for generations.

William turned and walked away, his coat snapped in the wind, a shadow severed from its source. She didn't move until he was gone. Then, with the same quiet authority she'd carried into the courtroom, she turned and descended the courthouse steps.

Judge Reid's ruling was more than a legal decision. It was a line drawn in the dirt and smoke of a town split between history and hunger. And as the courthouse emptied, the verdict echoed on—through alleys, across mineshafts, behind closed doors. The war had moved beyond the courtroom now.

This was no longer a case. It was a reckoning.

16

In the back room of The Copper Vein, the light was dim and low-slung, pooling beneath a single hanging bulb that cast long shadows against the walls. Smoke lingered like suspicion. Around the battered table, William sat with his closest men, the air between them thick with unsaid things.

"This farce in the courtroom," he growled, the words ground from between clenched teeth, "and now slander in the papers? It's a declaration of war."

Ethan nursed a whiskey, his jaw tight, his eyes rimmed red. "*The Butte Miner* fired me. Integrity, they said. As if any of them have a shred of it. They wanted blood, and I was the offering."

James leaned forward, arms on the table, his voice a cold cut through the smoke. "Then we stop defending. We go on the attack. Storar and her lawyer think they've won? Let's show them what happens when you back a predator into a corner."

Samuel nodded once. His silence had weight. "Talk is cheap. It's time we move. What's the play, William?"

He looked at each of them in turn, the flicker of the bulb carving hollows into his face. "Retribution," he said. The word dropped like iron. "Josephine Storar thinks her moral high ground makes her untouchable. Let's see how steady she stands when the ground shifts beneath her."

Ethan slammed his glass down. "I still have contacts. I can plant the right whispers—question her past, suggest the claim was never hers to begin with. Real or not, it won't matter. The doubt will take root."

James cracked his knuckles. "And Samuel and I can make sure her circle feels... less certain. Accidents happen. Messages get delivered."

Samuel's voice was low and precise. "We start small. Let the shadows do the talking."

William leaned back, a thin smile playing at his lips. "They want justice? We'll give them something else entirely."

The room fell quiet.

Later, when most had drifted off, Ethan remained slouched at the edge of the bar, the bottle half-empty beside him. James approached, eyes wary.

"Ethan, this isn't going to fix anything. Drowning it doesn't change what they took. But we're not finished.

Not yet."

He looked up, hollowed out. "They didn't just fire me, James. They erased me. The paper was my voice. Now all I've got is this." He lifted the glass.

"You still have us, and you've still got fight. Come on. Walk with me."

Outside, the night wrapped around them, sharp and wind-bitten. Butte slept with one eye open.

"I've lost my platform," he muttered. "Without it, who the hell am I?"

James didn't hesitate. "You're one of us. You know how to pull strings. Influence. We don't need the paper. We just need leverage. And I have a plan."

He glanced over. "I'm listening."

"We can't hit her directly. Too many eyes. But we can erode her. Undermine her claim, her reputation. Whisper scandal. Raise doubt."

He considered. "Rumors are air. They dissipate unless we weigh them down."

"That's your job. You know the town's back alleys better than anyone. We find dirt. And if there's none, we fabricate it. We make her question her own shadow."

They rounded a corner—and froze.

Ahead, under the yellow glow of a restaurant's front lanterns, Josephine and Phinnaeus Brandon stepped from the warmth into the brittle air.

Ethan stopped breathing.

She was radiant in the calm way that mocked his collapse. The soft click of her heels on the sidewalk might as well have been gunshots in his ears.

He stepped forward.

"Ethan," James hissed, grabbing his arm. "Not now. Not like this."

But something in him had already unraveled. The liquor, the humiliation, the coiled fury.

"No," he whispered, shaking him off. "I'm done watching."

They moved toward her car. Brandon opened the door. Josephine turned slightly, sensing them.

"Ethan Bennett," she said, her voice level. "To what do we owe this unexpected meeting?"

"You think you've won?" he spat. "You think you can ruin people and just walk away?"

His hand moved, sudden and final. The pistol glinted once under the streetlamp.

The crack of the shot tore through the quiet. Josephine staggered, blood blooming like a dark flower across her coat.

Brandon shouted, turned—and the second shot silenced him mid-motion.

They collapsed in tandem, two lives undone in a blink.

Screams rose from inside the restaurant, hands on windows, mouths agape.

James stood frozen.

"Ethan! Ethan! Come on. NOW!"

He looked down at what he'd done. The gun slipped from his fingers, landing with a dull thud on the pavement.

Then he ran.

James chased after him, their footsteps echoing down the empty street, louder than the gunshots, louder than the cries.

The night closed in around them like a noose.

And the reckoning had only begun.

17

They slipped into Butte's back alleys like fugitives from their own choices, the city folding in behind them—brick and soot and silence. The adrenaline that had once braced their limbs now fled, leaving a hollow ache in its wake. Cold sweat. Fraying nerves. The weight of two lives taken.

Inside the skeleton of an abandoned warehouse, where broken crates and rusted tools stood like monuments to a forgotten industry, Ethan collapsed onto a wooden pallet. The room was cavernous and still. Light filtered in through shattered windows, fractured and dust-hung.

James closed the door behind them, locking out the world. For a moment, neither spoke.

Then—"What the hell was that?" The words cut like steel, sharp and barely restrained. "Where did you get the gun, Ethan? How long have you been carrying it?"

He staggered to his feet, trembling with the aftershock. "It wasn't planned," he murmured. "I didn't mean for it to happen... not like that."

"You shot Josephine Storar," James said, slower now, as if saying it aloud might make it real. "And her lawyer. In front of a goddamn restaurant. In front of witnesses."

"I know," he choked. "I know, I know—" The words broke into sobs, guttural and raw, as he crumpled against the wall. "She took everything. My job, my name, my future. I saw her and... and it just—it just snapped."

James didn't answer right away. He crouched by a broken window, peering out at the flicker of passing headlights and the wail of distant sirens. "You didn't just snap. You pulled a trigger. Twice."

The silence that followed was suffocating.

"We need a plan," he said finally, standing. "This isn't just about you. This ties back to William. To the whole operation. You've made this bigger than either of us."

He wiped his face with a trembling hand, eyes wide with horror. "What if William finds out? What if he thinks I've jeopardized everything?"

"He will find out," James replied grimly. "But not yet. We need to get ahead of this."

A beat of fragile silence passed, broken only by the wind whistling through warped wood.

"I didn't mean to kill her," he whispered. "I just wanted her to hurt the way we've been hurting."

James stared at him. "And now the whole town's bleeding for it."

They sat in that warehouse like ghosts waiting for judgment, each sound from the street outside—a closing door, a cough, the crunch of gravel—amplified tenfold. The city, once their playground, had turned into a hunter. And they were the prey.

Across town, in the fire-lit belly of William's study, a storm was gathering.

He stood motionless as the news reached him. Then—

"Goddammit!" The whiskey glass shattered against the stone hearth, shards glittering like teeth. "He shot her? In public? In front of witnesses?"

The fire roared in reply. Samuel stood nearby, silent, a sentinel carved in shadow.

"This will bring everything down," he said, quieter now. "Everything."

Samuel nodded once. "We need to find them before the police do. If they talk—if they break—it's over."

"I'm not sending anyone, I'm going myself. We end this clean."

They moved like wolves through the night, slipping through alleys and side roads where no uniform dared wander. The town held its breath as they passed. Their boots scuffed the gravel, a dog barking and falling quiet. William's coat caught in the wind, the folds snapping behind him like a flag of war.

"I know where they'd go," Samuel said. "The old warehouse, the mill by the river—places they used to meet when things got tight."

William's eyes were sharp with memory. "If they've made me vulnerable," he said, voice a low rasp, "then I need to remind them who built this empire."

Meanwhile, in the chill hollow of the warehouse, Ethan sat against the wall, his face pale, his hands bloodless.

"We can't go to William," he muttered. "He'll kill me. You know he will."

"Maybe," James said, honest. "Or maybe he'll kill us both."

He turned to him. "We run?"

"And go where? You killed Josephine Storar. You killed her attorney. There's nowhere far enough."

Another siren cried in the distance. He flinched. James didn't.

"We wait till dawn," he said. "Then we choose."

A sudden gust of wind rattled the warehouse's warped frame. The air inside tasted like rust and endings.

William was coming. The law was coming. And the night, indifferent and watching, offered no mercy—

only consequence.

18

The cold predawn air was heavy with anticipation as William and Samuel arrived at the warehouse, a looming structure that seemed to stand as a silent witness to the countless stories hidden within. They exited their car with urgency, their footsteps crunching gravel as they approached the rusted door.

Samuel paused, hand on the handle, listening. Then he pushed it open.

Inside, the warehouse breathed dust and abandonment. Crates, collapsed machinery, and rusted chains lay strewn like relics of a forgotten age. Light filtered through shattered windows in fractured shafts. It was a graveyard of labor.

"James? Ethan?" William's voice rang out. Sharp. Commanding.

In the shadowed hollow of the warehouse, they stirred like men surfacing from a nightmare. The creak of the door. The footsteps. The voice they'd been dreading.

They rose.

When he saw them, his fury ignited like a struck match. "What the fuck were you thinking?" His voice thundered through the rafters. "You killed her? You shot Josephine Storar? In public? In front of witnesses?"

He flinched. "It wasn't planned," he stammered. "I didn't mean for it to happen... not like that."

James stood rigid, eyes wide, heart hammering.

Then William moved.

Not a yell this time—but a sudden, violent step forward. His fist curled, drawn halfway before he stopped himself. He almost didn't care. The crack of movement alone made Ethan stumble backward, bracing for impact that didn't come.

His hand hovered mid-air, trembling. His eyes burned.

And in that charged pause, the warehouse dissolved around them, replaced by memory.

For him, it was the cold judgment in his father's eyes —the suffocating pressure to be more, to be better, always better. Standing before William now, he felt it again: the shame, the panic, the paralyzing fear of being a disappointment too big to forgive.

For James, it was fists in the dark, the sting of the belt, the door slamming shut. William's fury was almost a perfect echo—controlled, precise, and just restrained enough to keep him guessing when the next blow might fall.

And then—
"Police! Don't move!"

The command cut through the air like a blade. William froze. All of them did.

In an instant, four officers swept into view. Two had flanked the warehouse from the rear. Guns raised. Voices firm.

Samuel didn't hesitate. He never did. When it came to protecting William, the line between muscle and murder blurred fast. In one brutal motion, he lunged, knocking one officer off balance. He wrenched the pistol from the other's grip and fired—once, then twice. The first officer dropped, blood blooming on his chest. The second collapsed in stunned silence.

Ethan and James dropped to the floor, clutching each other in sheer instinct. Dust rose around them, mingling with gun smoke and panic. Ethan's breath came in ragged gasps. James gripped his arm, a silent tether.

Another voice: "Put down your weapons!"

But William and Samuel were already firing. Bullets

ricocheted off beams, splitting silence into chaos.

"We gotta get out the back!" Samuel barked.

A beat passed. Then—

"Now!"

They bolted. Feet thundered over the warehouse floor. Shouts echoed behind them. Glass shattered.

They burst through the rear exit. The woods welcomed them like a trap sprung open.

Cool air slapped their faces. Leaves tore at their legs. Branches clawed their skin. But they ran—driven by the raw, animal urge to survive.

The canopy above fractured the first light of dawn, dappling the forest floor in trembling light. The town's cries fell away behind them, replaced by crickets and the hollow hoot of an owl.

Ethan gasped for breath, his side burning. James glanced back. Always glancing back.

They followed a path made by deer or desperation, until at last the trees thinned. A clearing opened like a wound. The sky above bled pink.

For one fleeting moment, they stood still.

In that quiet, they saw it—not redemption, not peace —but the illusion of distance. Of time. Of something other than doom.

But the woods were only a pause.

Beyond the trees, the reckoning waited. Patient. Unforgiving

19

E merging from the dense woods, the four men found themselves on the outskirts of Stonewood Mine, the looming structures casting long shadows in the blue-tinged hours before dawn. The mine, usually alive with the clang of machinery and the hum of men, now stood hollow, its silence unsettling. Only the ragged cadence of their breaths and the far-off barking of dogs broke the stillness—a brutal reminder that the hunt was not over.

William glanced over his shoulder at the trees they'd escaped, his voice tight. "This way."

They moved as one, their steps cautious, their presence spectral. At the edge of the equipment yard, the hushed glint of metal caught Samuel's eye. "There," he said, pointing to a weathered pickup truck tucked beneath the frame of a tin-roofed shelter.

The barking behind them surged, closer now. Urgency replaced caution. They broke into a sprint, gravel scuffing beneath boots. William reached the driver's side first, breath shallow, fingers fumbling beneath the visor. The keys dropped into his palm like a benediction.

Ethan threw one last glance behind them—the torchlight was flickering now, closing in. He and James scrambled into the truck bed, landing hard against sacks and rusted chains.

Samuel shoved into the driver's seat, elbowing William aside. The ignition coughed, caught, roared to life. They lurched forward, the truck fishtailing in loose gravel. Behind them, warning shots cracked through the air.

What followed was a blur—Butte unraveling in the rearview as the road unwound before them, tight-lipped silence threading the cab. In the back, Ethan stared skyward through a hole in the tarp, the stars like indifferent eyes.

Montana's broad shoulders carried them westward. The land stretched wide and wind-scoured, bearing witness to their flight. The ride to Missoula was punctuated by silence and the occasional snapped word from William, like lightning splitting a storm-dark sky.

Hidden beneath burlap and scrap in the bed, Ethan

and James found themselves more concealed than protected. The coarse weave scratched their skin, but it was the weight of thought that dug deepest. Neither spoke for some time. The drone of the tires became a kind of lullaby—soft, but laced with dread.

"Do you think we lost them?" James asked, breath shallow.

Ethan shifted, watching a sliver of day pry through the gap in their cover. "I don't know."

William's voice rose in the cab—harsh syllables flung at the windshield. What he said was obscured, but the tone carved through the truck like a blade.

"Do you think he knows?"

"Knows what? That we're scared?"

James sighed. "Yeah. That we're just... out of our depth."

The truck hit a rut, jostling them. James reached for Ethan's arm, grounding both of them.

"He might blame us," Ethan whispered. "For all of it."

"He might, but Samuel's still here. He balances the scales. Usually."

They let the wind speak for a while.

"I never pictured it ending like this. On the run."

"None of us did. But we played the game. Now we pay."

The cab held its own brand of storm. Samuel kept his hands steady on the wheel, cigarette on his lips, his voice a rasp of low, guarded words. He checked the rearview often—not just for pursuers, but to measure the men behind him.

"This is a mess, William. A real goddamn mess."

He didn't turn. "I know."

"The boys—they weren't ready. And now we've got blood on the road and law at our backs."

"Then we keep moving. Seattle. Canada. Whatever it takes. Butte was never the endgame."

"They're not cut out for this. They'll crack."

His stare finally found him. "Then they adapt. Or they don't. But they'll stay alive. That's the priority."

Samuel's fingers tapped the wheel, a rhythm born of nerves, not patience. He glanced into the rearview— at the tarp in the bed, the motionless humps of the boys beneath it. For a split second, something shifted behind his eyes. Not fear. Not regret. Something quieter.

Is this the last ride we take together?

The thought came and went like a breath he didn't dare speak aloud.

"They'll stay alive," he said again, firmer this time. But even he heard the echo of doubt in his voice.

The truck groaned over a stretch of broken asphalt. Their pact, forged in ambition, had become a yoke of necessity.

They reached Missoula by first light, hidden in the stillness that precedes waking. A derelict barn on the town's edge swallowed them. Its broken slats whispered in the wind.

James, returning from a brief lookout shift, dropped to a crouch inside the barn. "Saw two patrol cars roll slow through the edge of town. Didn't stop, but they're watching." That was all it took—Samuel reached for the map.

"We can't keep heading west. Seattle's crawling," he said.

Ethan rubbed his temples. "Then what? More hiding? More running?"

"We disappear deeper," James said. "Off-grid. For a while."

William pointed north. "We head to Great Falls. From there—we go to Canada."

Samuel frowned. "Canada? That's no short leap."

"It's our best chance. We lay low, regroup, and when it's time—we come back."

Ethan stirred uneasily. "It's a long shot. But staying here? It's suicide."

"We'll never cross clean," Samuel warned. "Not with the heat we're carrying."

James's voice was steady. "But it's something. It's not running—it's choosing something else."

The proposition of Canada, once a flicker of thought, now grew into a looming horizon. But as William laid out the plan, something subtle shifted in the space between them. The boys exchanged glances—uneasy, hesitant. The plan wasn't a choice. It was an order.

"So this is it, huh? On the run like rats," Ethan muttered, the exhaustion in his voice raw, unvarnished.

Samuel grunted, eyes on the dirt floor. "Rats survive, Ethan. That's what we've gotta do. Survive."

James leaned against the barn wall, arms crossed, gaze distant. "Survive for what? Another mine? Another scheme? We keep running, but the blood stays with us."

William's voice cut through, cold and decisive. "Canada's not the end. It's a means. We lay low, then we come back. We settle scores."

But the silence that followed was not agreement. It was something else—uncertainty, fatigue, the slow unraveling of conviction. James and Ethan weren't ready to keep following, not blindly. The ground beneath them no longer felt like a shared cause—it felt like being pulled.

Ethan looked at the map but didn't really see it. It felt less like a plan, more like a path someone else had chosen for him. "You really think we'll make it across? With everything that's happened? They're not just going to stop hunting us."

"Then we don't give them the chance," Samuel said, already gathering supplies. "We keep moving. We stay sharp. We do what we've always done."

James didn't answer. His jaw tensed. The image of Josephine's blood flashing again in his mind. He looked at Ethan—neither of them spoke, but the weight was shared. A weight that hadn't existed before that night. A weight that made every step forward feel like a betrayal of something they couldn't name.

Later, as they drove again, the engine a low, constant hum beneath their silence, Ethan turned to James. "You ever wonder if we're already lost?"

He didn't answer right away. Then: "More than I ever say."

The final leg of the escape felt less like motion, more like surrender. Each mile into the forest pulled them deeper from what they'd known, not toward something new, but away from everything broken.

They ditched the truck, melted into the woods. The trees closed around them. And ahead—north.

Canada loomed ahead, its mystery shrouded in the

unknown.

DJ ATKINSON

PART 2

DJ ATKINSON

20

The frost whispered first. Thin and lacy, it clung to the edges of the jack pine and poplar, a quiet warning stitched into bark and branch. Sheridan Lawrence paused on the narrow game trail, hand resting on the flank of his pack horse, breath fogging the morning air. A raven wheeled above, its cry sharp and solitary. The trail behind him was already fading beneath the dusting of snow. Ahead, the world narrowed into the hush of the woods.

He adjusted the leather strap across his shoulder and pressed on.

Each step was deliberate. Measured. At fifty-five, he moved with the kind of confidence carved by decades, not days. The weight he carried wasn't just food and tools—it was memory. Knowledge. Ghosts. The northern wild was not a place he visited; it was the rhythm to which he lived.

Born in 1870 in South Stukely, Quebec, he had learned early how to work the land, how to trust what a horse felt before it showed in its gait, how to listen to the seasons before they raised their voice. At sixteen, he'd followed his family west to the Peace River country—an expanse of unknown and unforgiving terrain that most men feared. They didn't.

By the turn of the century, he'd built something enduring on sixteen hundred acres near Fort Vermilion. Horses, cattle, hogs. Then came the flour mill. The sawmill. The dairy. A slaughterhouse. Not just for profit, but for survival. For sovereignty. He didn't just farm the land—he dared it to grow.

In 1900, he married Julia Scott. They called her Juey. Together, they raised fifteen children beneath a roof that smelled of woodsmoke and ambition. But in October, when the air began to taste metallic and the northern lights painted warnings across the sky, he left the world he'd built and returned to the one that had built him.

He packed light—tobacco, flour, oats, salt pork, traps —and saddled the same steady horse he'd used for years. From Fort Vermilion, he rode north to La Crête, where he'd leave the horse with friends. Then came the long walk: seventy-three miles on foot to the far end of his trap line, just south of Carcajou.

The journey took fourteen days, out and back. He walked six hours each day, sleeping in canvas tents or, when luck aligned with memory, the crude trap shacks he'd built along the way. Their walls were thin. Their comfort minimal. But each one held a stovepipe chimney and a stash of dry goods—proof against the cruel arithmetic of a northern freeze.

He hunted no trophies. He checked snares and leg holds, harvesting the life of the woods with practiced respect: beaver, lynx, wolf, muskrat, bobcat, coyote, otter. Sometimes weasel. Sometimes nothing. Each pelt hung in his hands with the weight of a bargain— one creature's life traded for his own endurance.

He did not speak much on the line. But when he passed through the Métis settlements or shared bannock with a Cree elder beside a fire, words came. Slowly. Like river ice breaking. There was trust there, built over seasons, not stories.

Now, in the hush of early winter, his children tended the farm, raised their own broods, their own dreams. The wilderness had become his alone again— a place not just of work, but of reckoning. The trees remembered him. The wind carried his name in the brittle branches.

A few weeks earlier, snow had dusted the region like flour on a butcher's apron. Just a taste of what was coming. He welcomed it. In the north, winter was not a punishment. It was a mirror.

This time, he moved slower. Not from weakness, but awareness. He marked the weight of his steps, the echo of each snapped twig, the tilt of light across the river's skin. It was not just about getting to the end of the line. It was about remembering why he went at all.

The trapline was a thread through the wilderness, yes —but it was also a thread through him. Each fall, he stepped away from the noise of machinery and the clatter of towns, and let the silence of snow and spruce unspool the man he'd become. Strip him down. Remind him.

This was his place. His rhythm. His way.

And though he walked alone, he was never without company. The land had a voice. And Sheridan Lawrence knew how to listen.

21

As the first light of dawn crept over the horizon, Sheridan stepped into the chill, his boots crunching over frost-laced earth. The breath from his nostrils rose in quiet plumes, drifting into the stillness. Autumn clung to the farm like a long-held note, its silence both peaceful and expectant. The barn loomed ahead, haloed in a faint silver mist.

From the farmhouse window, Juey watched his steady gait with an old ache stirring beneath her ribs. She clutched her shawl tighter, her breath fogging the glass. In her silence, there was love. And worry.

Inside, the kitchen hummed with warmth. Coffee bubbled gently on the stove, mingling with the scent of baking bread and smoke-softened wood. SHe turned to her daughter, Elizabeth, who had come home for this—just this—because they all knew the pattern, the rhythm of the leaving.

"He's determined as ever," she murmured, her voice nearly lost to the clatter of spoons and the low ticking of the wall clock.

Elizabeth looked toward the window, where dawn stretched itself slowly across the fields. "It's in him, Mama. The wild. It calls, and he listens."

She nodded, but her eyes didn't soften. "It calls louder every year, and I can't help but wonder... one day, it may not let him go."

Elizabeth didn't answer. Instead, she stepped closer, took her mother's hand—roughened from decades of work, yet warm. There were words between them, unspoken. It wasn't just distance that grew heavier each year—it was time.

Out at the barn, he moved with method, ticking through his list without writing a word. His sons, Michael and David had arrived early, their boots leaving fresh prints beside his in the thawing mud. They leaned on posts, hands buried in their coat pockets, watching him in silence.

"Pa," Michael said eventually, his voice carrying through the hay-dusted air. "You sure you've got enough packed? Feels colder this year already."

He didn't look up. His fingers were threading rope through his gloved hands, checking the strength of the knots. "I'm sure."

David stepped forward. "Let me come with you for the first few days. Just to set up."

He paused. The rope stilled.

For a moment, he didn't speak.

Then: "Appreciate it, boys. But this one's mine."

He lifted the rope, coiled it with a practiced flick. His voice was steady, but something in his eyes betrayed him—a flicker of hesitation, of gratitude left unspoken.

At the back of the barn, he reached for the snowshoes. The ash frames were worn smooth, the webbing tight. He traced one with a calloused thumb before unhooking it from the wall.

"Your granddad used these," he said. "Showed me how to bind them myself, said it could save your life one day."

Michael nodded. "They look ready for another hundred miles."

He smiled, but it didn't quite reach his eyes. "We'll see."

David leaned in, squinting at the worn leather. "You ever think about just staying home this year?"

The barn fell quiet.

He didn't answer right away. Instead, he adjusted the straps, checked the laces again. Finally, he stood, exhaling through his nose.

"Every year," he said. "And then I leave anyway."

Back in the kitchen, the women worked with a quiet efficiency. Dried fruit folded into bread. Jars of stew sealed with wax. Blocks of hard cheese and sausages wrapped in cloth.

"You think he knows we worry?" Elizabeth asked softly.

Juey didn't stop kneading. "Of course he does. He just carries it different. Turns it into something he can walk with."

Elizabeth placed the last jar into the canvas sack. "He walks a long way, Mama."

"I know, child." She wiped her hands and turned to face the table full of food. "That's why we pack it with everything but fear. He carries enough of that already."

Evening drew its long shadows across the floor as the men came in from the barn. The warmth of the kitchen, the smells, the table full of packed provisions —it was home in its truest form. A hearth without fire, a heart without words.

He looked at his family, at the bags of food, at her face.

"I'll leave first light," he said. "Keg River, then north. Should be back in a month. Maybe a week more."

She met his gaze. "And if not?"

His reply came quick, practiced. "Then come looking."

But this time, the old joke didn't land. Elizabeth glanced down.His sons shifted. The silence that followed was not unfamiliar—but this year, it felt heavier.

Sheridan moved toward Juey and put his arms around her. She leaned back into him.

"You always come back," she said.

He held her tight. "I do."

But neither of them said what they both felt.

That something in the air was different this time.

The night closed in. They ate together, laughed lightly, shared stories from summers past. But even the fire in the hearth seemed quieter.

When he rose to turn in, they rose with him. One last embrace. One last look.

Outside, frost had returned to the fields. In the window, Juey watched his silhouette move through the dark, lantern in hand. She couldn't name it, but the wind felt heavier this year.

She didn't cry. Not yet.

But she stood there a long while, long after the light was gone.

22

As the first tendrils of dawn stretched across the sky, painting the horizon with strokes of pink and gold, Sheridan stood at the threshold of departure. The air was crisp, filled with the scent of pine and the earthy musk of autumn leaves—a herald of the winter to come. The homestead, bathed in the early light, was a tableau of tranquility, its daily rhythms still asleep.

Today marked the commencement of his annual sojourn into the wilderness, a pilgrimage as intrinsic to his soul as the very air he breathed. The trap line awaited him, a call to adventure and introspection.

In the quietude of the barn, he meticulously prepared his supplies, each item a companion on the journey ahead. From the well-worn traps and snares to the clean, reliable rifle, every piece was a testament to his deep connection and respect for the wilderness.

Outside, Belle, his faithful mare, stood ready, her breath visible in the morning chill. Their bond was one of silent understanding, a partnership honed through seasons of shared paths and challenges.

The sun's rays began to illuminate the homestead. As he tightened the last strap on his pack, the sound of footsteps approached softly over frost-laced earth. He turned to find Juey standing at the barn door, wrapped in her shawl, a Thermos of hot coffee tucked against her chest.

"I thought you might need this," she said, stepping inside. Her voice was hushed, as if raising it too loud might wake something neither of them wanted disturbed.

He smiled and took it from her hands, their fingers brushing. "You know me too well."

"I ought to, after all these years." Her eyes shimmered in the pale morning light. "I didn't sleep much."

"I know," he said softly. "I didn't either."

She watched him for a moment, then reached out and adjusted the collar of his coat. Her touch lingered longer than usual.

"I packed the red scarf," she said. "The one you always forget."

"I noticed," he murmured, eyes crinkling with a smile. "I'll wear it. Every day."

There was a pause, filled only by Belle's soft exhale and the distant crackle of waking birds.

"Come back," she whispered.

"Always," he replied. And then, as if afraid the words might unravel, he kissed her—gently, reverently. A promise passed between them, wordless and weighty.

She stepped back, her eyes never leaving his. "We'll be waiting."

He gave a quiet nod, then turned toward Belle, hoisting his pack with practiced ease. As he mounted, he looked back one last time. She stood just beyond the doorway now, framed in the golden light, a still point in the turning world.

The barn door swung open, and with a soft nudge to Belle, he set off. His route beckoned, but Juey's love—the warmth of it, the ache of it—followed him into the trees.

His journey to La Crête, a twenty-eight mile ride through the dense boreal forest of northern Alberta, began. Belle moved confidently beneath him, her hooves making soft sounds on the forest floor, muffled by the thick layer of fallen needles and leaves. The path they followed was familiar, yet each journey revealed the forest in a new light, especially now, as the season teetered on the edge of winter's embrace.

This forest, with its dense canopy of coniferous and deciduous trees, was more than a mere backdrop to his life; it was a repository of knowledge and skill, a heritage passed down from his father and now to his sons and grandchildren.

His father had taught him to read the forest as one would read a book, seeing not just trees but the potential for survival and ingenuity. Each species of tree, each underbrush plant, held a specific purpose that went beyond its immediate appearance. The Black Spruce and Balsam Fir, with their sturdy boughs, were not just part of the landscape but materials for snares that could hold fast in the coldest winters. This knowledge was second nature to him, as ingrained in him as the lines on his palms.

Riding through the forest, his eyes moved over the familiar terrain with a practiced ease. The Jack Pine and Paper Birch, each unique in its growth, offered themselves as resources for trap-making—a technique his father had mastered and passed on to him. The birch's peeling bark could be fashioned into cords, while the resin of the poplar was a natural adhesive, invaluable in the wilderness.

As Belle navigated the path, he reflected on the lessons he had imparted to his own sons and grandchildren. The flexible willows and the nitrogen-fixing alders by the water's edge were more than just plants; they were lessons in adaptability and sustainability.

The understory, rich with bush cranberry and lined with mosses and lichens, was a testament to the forest's bounty. He had taught his children to see the value in every part of this ecosystem, from the berries that could sustain them through long winters to the moss that could camouflage their snares.

This journey, like many before it, was a silent dialogue between him and the land—a dialogue that spoke of respect, understanding, and the continuity of knowledge across generations. The skills his father had taught him, which he, in turn, had passed to his sons and grandchildren, were not just techniques for survival; they were a legacy of living in harmony with the natural world. The knowledge of how to use the forest's resources to craft snares and traps was a part of him, as natural as breathing.

Fifteen miles into his journey, they arrived at the first of his five shacks scattered along his circuit. This shack, a sturdy structure built from the very timber it stood amongst, served as a testament to his craftsmanship. It appeared as a welcoming silhouette against the encroaching evening, its simple design harmonizing with the surrounding environment.

He slid off his horse with the familiarity of long years in the saddle, though he felt the stiffness of the day's ride settling into his bones. He led her to a makeshift corral beside his shack—a humble enclosure crafted from interwoven branches and rope spun from the fibrous bark of the Paper Birch. He carefully removed her saddle and bridle, and began to brush her down, making sure she was comfortable after their journey. Nearby, a small stream offered fresh water, which he collected in a bucket for her to drink, then supplied some oats from his supplies to feed her for the evening.

With her settled, he turned his attention to his shack. He unlocked the heavy wooden door, its hinges groaning softly as it swung open, revealing the interior. It was sparsely furnished, containing only the essentials: a wooden cot with a thick, woolen blanket, a sturdy table and chair, and a fireplace built from river stones collected from the nearby stream.

He quickly set to work lighting the fire, gathering the dry, crackling kindling he had prepped from Trembling Aspen and Jack Pine. The flames caught eagerly, spreading warmth and illumination throughout the small cabin, a welcome barrier against the encroaching evening chill. Over the lively fire, he placed a pot of water, and soon the comforting aroma of stew—made from provisions Juey and Elizabeth had thoughtfully packed—began to fill the air.

As the stew simmered, he unfolded his cot, arranging his sleeping space for the night with methodical care. Seated at the table with his humble meal, he pondered the tasks for the following day. Planning to extend his stay by another night, he intended to use the time to strategically set traps and snares around the area. His mind mapped out the specifics of each trap, designed to cater to the habits of various local wildlife such as raccoons, wolves, otters, beavers, lynxes, bobcats, coyotes, weasels, and muskrats, ensuring his efforts would be as effective as possible.

One ingenious trap he planned to set was a modified figure-four deadfall, using a heavy log balanced precariously on a trigger mechanism made from the sturdy branches of Balsam Fir. This trap would be ideal for larger animals like lynx or coyote, its design ensuring a humane and swift capture.

For the smaller, more elusive creatures like weasels and muskrats, he would employ snares crafted from the strong, flexible fibers of Paper Birch bark. These snares would be placed along known animal trails, camouflaged with moss and leaves to blend seamlessly into the forest floor.

Another trap, a simple pitfall covered with a lattice of Jack Pine branches and a thin layer of forest detritus, would be dug near the stream for otter or beaver. The water's edge, a natural pathway for these animals, provided the perfect location for such a trap.

As he ate, he reflected on the necessity of these traps, not just for sustenance but as a practice of his skills and a continuation of the legacy passed down from his father. These traps, though empty now, would be checked on his return journey, a cycle of preparation and harvest that mirrored the rhythms of the wilderness itself.

The evening passed into night, and wrapped in the quiet of the forest and the warmth of the fire, he considered the future. The skills he honed here, the traps he set, were not just for the animals of the forest. He didn't know yet what shape that prey might take. But he would be ready.

23

The autumn day rose sharp and clean, its chill edged in promise. He stepped into the woods at first light, boots pressing softly against a forest floor blanketed in gold and crimson. Overhead, the canopy filtered the sun in ribbons. The world smelled of frost and earth, of endings.

He moved with quiet purpose, the weight of the traps across his back familiar, each step a practiced echo of years gone by. Along a ridge, he knelt to carve figure-four triggers from green Balsam Fir, his knife biting cleanly through the grain. The logs he selected were heavy, balanced with the same precision he gave his rifle. Once set, they disappeared into the landscape, silent mechanisms waiting for motion.

Further down, he turned to the smaller work—snares for weasel, muskrat, rabbit. He stripped bark from Paper Birch, his fingers nimble, and laid the loops along narrow trails, masked beneath moss and fallen leaves. There was a reverence in the task. Not conquest—never that—but an understanding.

By midday, the sun hung pale above the treetops. He moved toward the stream, where animal tracks braided through soft ground and shadow. The place held promise—but hid peril too. He meant to set a pitfall near the water's edge, where otter and beaver often passed. But as he stepped across the leaf-littered marsh, the ground gave way.

In an instant, he was sinking—thigh-deep in mud, the cold biting into his legs, the suction pulling. Panic flared, sharp and primal. For a moment, his mind flashed not to tools or timber, but to Juey. The feel of her hand that morning. The red scarf. Would she ever know how hard he fought? How close he came to vanishing? His legs thrashed, heavier than they once were. His strength no longer limitless. He wasn't afraid of dying—but of being buried where no one would know how hard he'd fought to live.

He closed his eyes. Let breath steady the thrum of blood in his ears. Instinct, not fear.

Alder. Willow.

He remembered the roots, the strength in their tangle.

Straining, he reached for a nearby branch, then another. He wove them into a crude lattice, careful and slow, a net across the muck. With effort, he shifted his weight, inching across the frame, pulling free limb by limb. The marsh released him like a reluctant memory.

Flat on the forest floor, chest heaving, he lay still. The cold had teeth. The silence pressed in.

He thought of his children—grown, scattered like leaves—and how none of them would know how close he'd just come. How far he'd drifted from being found.

He rolled to his side, coughing up a breath that felt half-laugh, half-prayer. He would tell no one. But he would remember.

Mud clung to him like shadow, but he was whole. Alive. Another test endured—but not without cost.

He rose, gathered his tools, and set the pitfall all the same—wiser now to the marsh's false face. More wary of the land's casual cruelty.

When he returned to the shack, twilight was already slipping through the trees. The mud on his boots and trousers bore its own story. Inside, he set a pot on the fire, stripped off his clothes, and scraped the muck away with a shard of bark. The work was steadying. Restorative.

With the water heated, he scrubbed with homemade soap, the scent clean and sharp, mingling with pine smoke. He rinsed his garments in the stream, hung them to dry by the hearth, then turned to supper. The stew was warm, the fruit bread dense and sweet—a tether to home.

Each bite held the echo of Juey's voice, her hands kneading warmth into the dough, her quiet insistence on love. And tonight, more than usual, it held something else.

A reason to come back.

Morning came clear. Frost coated the world like fine sugar. He checked Belle, fed her oats, and saddled her once more. The traps now lay behind, silent witnesses to his presence.

The ride to La Crête passed through changing woods—conifer to mixed brush, the hush of forest giving way to wider light. He remained alert, scanning the trees not with fear, but with attentiveness honed by time.

Henri Beaumont's homestead appeared just past noon, settled into a sunlit clearing. Henri waited outside, his frame lean, still, but his grin uncontained.

"Sheridan, old fox! You made it."

Belle nickered. Henri held out a hand full of oats. She pressed her muzzle into his palm.

Sheridan dismounted. "She remembers everything. I do too. Thanks for keeping her safe."

He clapped his shoulder. "Madeleine's inside. Dinner's nearly ready. She's been fussing like you were royalty."

Inside, warmth. Lantern light. The scent of stew, bread, and roasting meat. Children's laughter. She embraced him with flour-dusted hands.

"Welcome, Sheridan. You look thinner than last year."

He smiled. "That's the forest's doing."

At dinner, stories flowed. He spoke of his ride, the traps, the mud. The children leaned close, wide-eyed.

Then Henri grew serious. "There's a wolf pack nearby. Bigger. Bolder. Too close to town."

Madeleine added, "A friend of mine—been trapping longer than most—said they came in the night. Took everything. Left claw marks in the canvas. Not even afraid of fire."

He listened. Nodded. "I'll shift my traps. Stay alert."

Henri met his gaze. "Do more than stay alert. Trust the wild. It's not just hunger, Sheridan. Something's off. They're watching longer. Closer."

The fire crackled. The talk turned lighter, but the warning settled like a weight in the room.

That night, he lay in the guest cot, the scent of woodsmoke in the rafters, the murmur of the forest just beyond the walls. The trapline waited. So did the wolves. But something else stirred—just beneath thought. Not fear. A shift. The wilderness was changing. And somewhere inside, so was he.

24

Morning came cold and clear, a steel thread of winter stitched into the light. At the Beaumont homestead, the warmth of firelight spilled across the kitchen floor. Coffee percolated low and steady, and the scent of baking— butter, flour, spice—lifted into the rafters. Madeleine, hands dusted in flour, worked dough with the care of ritual, pressing it into the familiar tin of a Tourtière.

Sheridan stepped inside, the door closing softly behind him. He didn't speak at first; the smells, the heat, the simplicity of the moment caught him. She glanced up, offered a nod and a kind smile.

"Thought you might carry some warmth with you," she said, gesturing to the pie cooling by the window, beside a parcel wrapped in waxed cloth. He nodded. "Your cooking might be the thing that keeps the frost off my back."

Henri joined them, shoulders squared, gaze steady. "You're heading into the heart of it now. The land listens. Stay sharp."

He clasped his hand. "And Belle?"

"She'll be here, rested and fattened when you return. Count on it. Just be sure you do."

He smiled. Brief. Heavy. Then he crossed the yard and found Belle waiting, tethered near the fence, her breath rising in soft puffs. He ran his hand along her neck.

"Rest easy, girl. We've still got roads ahead."

She leaned into his touch. It was the closest she came to a goodbye.

With Madeleine's provisions secured, he slung the pack over his shoulder, its weight a comfort. "I'll be back," he said. "Hungry, I expect."

"We'll be waiting," she replied, her voice low.

And then he was gone, walking alone into the hush of pine and spruce.

The first hour passed in a rhythm of breath and bootfall. The pack shifted awkwardly at his back. He paused beneath a stand of fir, unshouldered it, and dug through until his fingers touched something unexpected: a slingshot. His youngest must have tucked it in, a child's farewell in rubber and carved wood. He repositioned it gently, then continued on, a small smile flickering and gone.

His stride lengthened. The forest accepted him, swallowed his sound. Needles and leaves softened each step. Ten, maybe fifteen miles ahead. He walked with purpose, but not urgency. The land allowed no haste.

Four hours in, something changed. The light shifted. The quiet deepened. And a feeling—thin, unmistakable—rose at the base of his spine. Watched. Not seen, but felt. He stopped. Scanned the trees. No sound, no movement. But the forest had drawn its breath.

His hand closed around the knife. Not for use—just to remember it was there. He waited. Nothing. Just the echo of Henri's voice in his mind, and the ancient instinct that still stirred beneath his ribs.

He altered his course. Chose higher ground, clearer sightlines. Thought through what he knew: how to look larger, how to make noise without sounding afraid. The feeling ebbed, but never left entirely.

Seven hours passed. The light stretched long and gold. The air thinned with cold. He neared a familiar clearing—flat ground, close to water. He scanned it, then nodded. It would do.

First, he hung the food high, roped in the crook of an old spruce. The tent came next: tight canvas, low to the ground, back to a thicket of evergreens. Windbreak. Then the fire, coaxed from dry pine and flint. Its warmth pushed against the falling dark.

He placed the Tourtière near the flames. The scent rose slow and rich, mingling with woodsmoke. For a moment, the forest seemed to lean in.

At the stream, he knelt to fill his pot. The mud was soft, the banks dark with moisture. And there: tracks. Broad. Deep. Wolf.

He followed them with his eyes. Single file, then fanned out. Clever. Masked their number. The fire behind him felt suddenly small.

He returned to camp and laid out his tools. The knife. The slingshot. Smooth stone ready in the cradle. Not much. But enough to feel like choice. He wouldn't set traps for wolves. He didn't hunt what watched.

He fed the fire more wood, building it higher. Its light stretched into the trees, uncertain.

As the first howl threaded through the dark, he sat cross-legged by the flames. Not afraid. Not entirely. The wild had shifted. That much he knew.

But so had he.

25

D awn broke clean and pale, a muted gold behind the spruce. The fire had gone to coals. He rose from his bedroll, stiffness settling in his joints like sediment. No need for a fire this morning. The air bit but didn't wound. He packed with quiet efficiency, the memory of last night's wolf tracks lingering but not enough to cloud him. Today, he was heading somewhere different. Somewhere that felt like home.

The path led north by northwest, a narrow, winding line through frost-touched undergrowth. Familiar. His family's cabin stood on a bluff above the Peace River, its walls weathered but strong, its silence filled with echoes. He'd made this walk a hundred times. Maybe more.

With every step, the forest opened wider, and the river came into view, glinting beneath the wide Alberta sky.

145

Its surface was calm, mirroring clouds that drifted like thoughts. He knew the D.A. Thomas would soon tie up for the winter, the river surrendering to ice. Until then, it still moved.

By late morning, the cabin appeared—framed in birch and cedar. Larger than the trapline shacks, it bore the fingerprints of summers past—his sons, his grandchildren, laughter sealed into the wood grain. Built not just to endure, but to hold.

Inside, dust and woodsmoke lingered. The stove stood like an old friend, patient and cold. A match flared; flames took hold, and soon water was heating. Coffee grounds met the boil, scent rising like memory itself. Warmth crept into the space, curling into corners, loosening something in his chest.

Memories of his father stirred with the steam from the mug. Fishing lines pulled taut along this river. Lessons passed without words—just a glance, a nod, a stillness that said more than speech. How to read a current. Walk without sound. Listen until the land spoke back.

A summer morning returned to him—not long ago. His youngest grandson, bare-chested and fearless, had waded straight into the river, ignoring his mother's protests. On the bank, coffee in hand, he had feigned disapproval, eyes narrowed over the rim of the cup, though the smile behind it was impossible to hide. The boy had slipped, splashed, come up sputtering and grinning. Later, they'd carved a driftwood stick into a fishing rod together, casting it again and again into the current. Not to catch, but to learn.

Now he stayed for two nights. He would fish. Check old traps by the water. Not to take, but to touch the rhythm again. The Peace unraveled things in him he didn't know he'd tied so tight. He sat with his coffee and watched the water move.

By noon, he'd tidied the cabin and walked the narrow trail down to the riverbank, where the log seats still waited. Tackle in one hand. Bait in the other. Memory in every step. Three hundred yards downstream, a moose broke the tree line, stepped into the shallows, and drank. He watched, still. Humbled.

The canoe rested nearby, turned upside-down beside the thicket. Last summer, the place had teemed with noise. His grandchildren on horseback, the clatter of gear, Madeleine's stew heating on the stove, the thunk of boots on porch steps. Today, silence held court.

The absence pressed in—familiar, but sharper than before.

He couldn't say why it weighed more this time. Why 'the quiet' was louder. He didn't try to name it. He fished instead. Cast after cast. Hands remembering.

Later, he walked the edge of the river, checking the old sets. Most needed repair. He marked their locations. Tomorrow, he'd return with fresh cord and wire. He moved slowly. Deliberately. Not out of fatigue, but respect.

Dinner was what the river gave—a grayling, fat with the season. He cooked it over the stove flame, with dry goods from a metal box his daughter had filled. Canned tomatoes. Biscuits in wax paper. Love, sealed up tight.

Night fell quick. The fire warmed the cabin and pushed back the dark. He cleaned the pot, washed his cup, and set them on the rack, the clink of enamel a sound he knew by heart.

The handmade bed welcomed him, built board by board with his sons, each board nailed with care. The blankets were soft. Heavy with memory.

Outside, the trees moved. Branches tapped. Wind slid through the timber like a whisper.

Then, the sound. Low and distant. A howl. Then more. Threaded yaps. Wolves, far off. Talking in the night.

He listened. Not afraid. Not welcome, either. But part of it. Part of all of it.

He remembered his grandson once asking, "Do the wolves ever come this close?" The boy had whispered it beneath the blankets, eyes wide, half-hoping for yes.

His eyes closed. The wolves called again, somewhere deep beyond the river. And Sheridan slept, not alone in the silence, but folded inside it.

26

The cold met his skin like breath drawn through teeth—sharp, immediate, honest. Dawn crept in slow through the cabin windows, brushing frost from the panes with pale light. He rose without groan or fuss, every motion shaped by years of mornings just like this. The stove sat dormant in the center of the room, and with practiced ease he brought it back to life, coaxing flames from kindling as though whispering old secrets.

A pot of water went on. Soon the bubbling murmur began, and with it, the scent of coffee—earthy, anchoring. It mingled with the resin of pine smoke curling from the stove. These were the sounds and smells that built a man's day, stone by stone.

Mug in hand, he stepped outside. Snow, faint and fresh, had settled in the night. It crunched softly underfoot, a delicate crust breaking beneath his

boots. Then he saw them: the tracks. Crisp outlines encircling the cabin, dark against the white.

Wolves.

Their prints moved from the cover of trees to the open, then scattered outward—a single file unraveling into many. He crouched, studying them. Curiosity had drawn them close. Hunger, maybe. Winter was coming hard this year, and even predators grew bold in the lean weeks.

He didn't fear them. But the message was clear.

Back inside, he finished his coffee, mind working. The wolves had watched. Not far. Not long ago. It shifted something in him—not alarm, exactly, but a heightening.

He spent the morning walking the trap line, deliberate and light-footed. The first—a deadfall—was built low near a game trail. He carved the trigger smooth, positioned the bait, balanced the weight just so. Intended for rabbit or marten. Not wolves.

Further down, he placed a snare. Wire looped with care, half-hidden beneath leaves. The work was precise, respectful. He set nothing with malice. Only intent. And always, his eye strayed to the edges of the trees.

By midday the sun softened the snow's crust, footprints fading into slush. The land, as always, moved on.

The rest of the day, he gave to the river.

His gear was simple. Familiar. A rod worn by weather and use. Bait kept in a cloth pouch. He followed the slope down to the broad bend, where slow water pooled beneath cottonwoods. Hand-cut benches still waited where they'd been set seasons ago.

He cast. The lure slipped beneath the surface, vanished without fuss. Fishing here wasn't always about hunger. Sometimes it was about remembering.

He settled onto a bench, rod in hand, sun brushing his shoulders. The river talked in ripples and wind. A hawk circled once, then vanished into light. For a while, everything held.

Then—a shift.

The forest offered no sound. Still, he knew.

He looked up. Three hundred yards downriver, a shape stood between trees.

Grey.

Still.

The wolf watched him. Not crouched. Not afraid. Just... there. Regal. Whole. The distance was vast, and yet something passed between them—recognition without name.

No move to flee. No move to advance. Only eyes, level and dark, holding.

He didn't move either.

The wolf turned first. Faded, quiet as breath, into the trees.

He watched until the last flick of tail disappeared.

Back at the cabin, he cleaned his trout and cooked it slow over flame. Dry goods joined it—canned tomatoes, the last of the biscuits his daughter packed. Provisions packed by loving hands. Every bite, a tether.

The light outside dimmed. The stove burned warm. Shadows pressed gently against the windows.

He sat for a while, cup in hand, replaying the day.

The work. The wolf. The river.

And when sleep came, it came easy.

Outside, somewhere deep in the woods, a howl answered the night. Not a threat. Not a warning. Just presence.

He didn't wake.

He was already part of it.

27

The day began the way they all did: quietly, deliberately. Coffee grounds stirred into boiling water, steam rising like breath from the lip of the pot. The cabin held onto the last of the night's cold, its silence undisturbed but for the soft clink of tin against the stove and the shuffle of boot soles on plank. He moved through the motions with the ease of habit, each act a thread in the larger fabric of his solitude.

After eating, he cleaned the space, folding his blanket, wiping crumbs from the table, tucking supplies away with the same care he'd shown building this life. It was reverence, not routine. Respect for the four walls that had kept him warm. Outside, the day waited.

With his pack slung across his shoulders, he stepped into the crisp air. The trail stretched ahead—fifteen miles to his third shack. A shift of place, but not of

purpose.

The forest greeted him with familiar grace: spruce and pine arching overhead, branches sighing with the weight of morning. Gold light split the canopy in slender ribbons, brushing the frost-laced undergrowth. The last of the autumn leaves curled beneath his boots. Somewhere, a loon called once—distant, hollow—a bell tolled in an empty church.

He worked the line with practiced care, eyes sweeping the ground, hands crafting traps with an artisan's touch. Each snare set low, each trigger whittled clean. There was no haste, no waste. Only attentiveness. Only the land.

Midway through the journey, the rhythm broke. Tracks—Not one—many. Their prints threaded across the trail, purposeful and clean. Intermixed with them: moose. The signs told a story, and he followed it, cutting into denser brush. The hush here was deeper. The air held something.

He followed.

Through dense alder and frozen brush, the path told its story. Snow scuffed, saplings broken. Then blood—scattered at first, then pooling. And ahead, the carcass.

A moose, half-draped in ravens.

The birds shrieked and lifted as he approached. The kill was fresh. The wolves had fed recently. Efficient. Hungry. The moose might've been the one from the

river—the one he'd watched drink just days ago. That idea sat in him like a stone.

He told himself it was better they'd fed. Less likely to roam close again. Still, when he reached the next shack, his fingers checked the latch twice.

He crouched near the edge of the clearing. The forest was still. The work was done. Nothing but remains.

He thought of his grandson again—the one always asking questions. "Do animals grieve? Do they remember?" The boy had asked once, eyes wide, serious in a way only children could be. They'd been sitting on the cabin step, eating salted peanuts. The question had outlasted the snack. He hadn't known how to answer then. He still didn't.

He left the wolves in their silence. The ravens returned before he'd gone twenty paces.

By late afternoon, the sun began to fall, washing the trees in copper and violet. The third shack came into view like a memory—a small shape against the expanse. One room. A stove. A place to rest.

He stepped inside and shut the door behind him. Cold clung to the walls, but it wouldn't last. He lit the stove and fed it patiently. The crackle of flame answered back, steady and sure.

Supplies came next: canned beans, jerky, oatmeal, and dry staples. He unpacked slowly, hands remembering the rhythm. Every tin, every paper-wrapped parcel bore the invisible fingerprints of home. His daughter had packed most of them. He could still hear her voice —"Don't eat it all in one night, Dad."

Dinner was modest. Just enough. Conservation came naturally—always had.

Later, he laid out his route for the next day, tracing a mental map he knew better than any drawn one. He made notes, scratched lines on a scrap of birch bark. His traps would need to adapt. So would he.

As the fire warmed the small room and the outside darkened, he wrapped himself in thick blankets, settling onto the narrow bunk.

But sleep hesitated.

He wasn't unsettled. Not exactly. Just aware. More than usual. The kill site had shifted something. So had the tracks circling the second cabin. He'd double-latched the door tonight. Habit, maybe.

Or something else.

Beyond the walls, the forest hummed. An owl called, low and distant. Wind moved through the high boughs.

He let it all in. Every sound, every silence. He belonged to it now.

Tomorrow would come with its own trials. But for now, wrapped in warmth, he lay still.

A branch creaked. Snow shifted on the roof. He

listened, and the night listened back.

28

Dawn broke quietly, and he rose into it like a man returning to something sacred. Light edged the frost-slicked window, silvering the glass as it rose. He stirred from his blankets slowly, the cold brushing his skin like breath from a forgotten world.

The ache in his back, the weight in his limbs—these were not complaints, but markers. Evidence of days well spent. He stretched, then stoked the stove. Wood, flame, breath. The crackle was low and sure, the warmth that followed gradual and clean. Fire as a companion. A confession.

Then came coffee—the scent rich, grounding, curling through the cabin like a familiar song, anchoring him. He sipped by the window, watching the morning unfurl beyond the pane—soft birdsong threading through the underbrush, light catching in the frost-laced pines, a world waking at its own rhythm.

After breakfast, he tidied the small room with the same deliberate grace. Every dish washed, every item in place. Not habit. Devotion. Then the door shut behind him, and the forest took him back.

The traps waited.

Map and compass in hand, he moved through the hush of the trees. The sun climbed higher, spilling light through the canopy. Where it touched the ground, the leaves burned gold and rust. His boots whispered across the forest floor, carrying him into the quiet work.

Each snare he inspected was a study in tension and trust. Wire, held just so. Bait, placed with care. He reset what needed resetting. Replaced what had worn thin. The traps weren't about conquest—they were conversation. The land set the rules.

Mid-morning brought a shift.

A rustle, faint. Footfalls too measured to be animal. He paused, listening.

Ahanu.

The man stepped from the trees with the ease of someone who belonged. His silhouette was lean, his presence calm.

"Ahanu," he called, warmth surfacing. "Good to see you, my friend. What brings you out this way?"

Ahanu's smile broke slowly. "Following the trail. Checking on the land. Thought I might cross your path."

They clasped hands—more than greeting. A bond worn smooth by seasons.

"Busy with the line," Sheridan said, nodding to the snare he'd just finished. "Getting ready for the cold. How's everything at the settlement?"

"Good. The way it always is before winter. Preparations, stories, births, goodbyes. The usual turning."

He smiled again, eyes warm with memory. "But tell me—when was the last time you sat around a fire with us? You should come tomorrow night. Food, fire, stories. My wife's been perfecting something new. I think she's hoping you'll show."

The offer warmed something quiet in him—a part too long untouched by voices not his own.

"I'd like that," he said. "It's been too long. The forest is good company, but it doesn't laugh the same way people do."

They talked for a while—about hunts gone sideways, the old men who told better lies than truths, children born into a world still learning how to hold them.

Their talk meandered like meltwater—winding, unhurried, finding old channels beneath the thaw.

Ahanu brought news from the settlement—recent gatherings, the joy of new life, the quiet sorrow of elders passing on. And through it all, the pulse of their shared respect for the land.

Before parting, Ahanu placed a hand on his shoulder.

"I'm looking forward to tomorrow, my friend. Safe travels. And don't let those traps outsmart you," he added, grinning.

Sheridan chuckled. "Not if I can help it. See you then."

As Ahanu disappeared into the woods, blending with the trees, Sheridan stood for a long moment, watching. Then he turned back to the work.

The snares felt different now. Not just tools, but symbols—of balance, of heritage, of a shared pact with the land. The task no lighter, but somehow more whole.

He worked on, the forest breathing steady beside him. With warmth and stories waiting beyond the trees, the day folded gently inward, like hands closing around flame.

29

The settlement unfolded around him, alive with rhythm and work. It was a world apart from the silence of the woods—children laughing, dogs darting, voices lifted in the cadence of task and conversation. Nets were mended by sure hands, tools sharpened with care, fires tended with reverence. Everything here bore the mark of necessity and kinship. No excess. No waste.

As he moved deeper, nods greeted him—familiar, unspoken acknowledgments that needed no words. The dogs trailed him, curious and joyful, weaving between his legs like shadows with heartbeat. This was a place that moved together, each body a thread in the wider weave.

The air held the scent of smoked meat and fresh earth, of hides stretched taut in the sun and stew simmering low. Autumn's edge was near, and the settlement moved with it—preparing, preserving, enduring. Amid it all: laughter. The light kind that came from a place of knowing. The kind that had seen hardship and still chose joy.

Ahanu approached, smile wide and easy.

"Sheridan! You've made it," he said, clapping a hand to his shoulder, guiding him toward the family home. The structure, simple but beautiful, stood firm in the land, as though it had grown there.

Inside, warmth greeted him. Miakoda, serene and steady, nodded her welcome.

"It's good to see you again, Miakoda," he said. His eyes dropped to the boys. "And look at how much Chayton and Elan have grown!"

She smiled, pride softening the lines of her face. "They've shot up like spring saplings, haven't they?"

He crouched low, grinning. "Last time I was here, I think you two were just able to peek over the table."

The boys giggled, bashful, then held up a small wooden canoe, their latest project.

He turned it over in his hands. "You've done good work," he said. "Fine hands. Fine minds."

She nodded, eyes reflecting gratitude—and something quieter. "We do our best. The boys are learning fast—fishing, tracking, even reading from those books you brought last time."

He glanced around the home. Woven hangings lined the walls, tools placed just so, everything worn by use and love. A life close to the land. Nothing false.

Ahanu gestured to the table. "You've come at a good time. We're preparing for a feast tonight. Giving thanks for what the land has offered."

His breath caught slightly at the scent—woodsmoke and spice settling deep in his chest. "I'm honored to be here. The walk through the woods always reminds me what matters. And this place—it does the same."

Miakoda smiled gently. "Your visits remind us that respect for the land has many forms. That we're not alone in how we see the world."

As they settled, he shared what he could. Spoke of his wife—her steadiness, her laughter. Of the rivers swollen with trout. Of quiet mornings and full nets.

But then his tone shifted.

"Came across a moose, not far from here. Brought down by wolves. It wasn't long dead. Tracks around my cabin too. They've been bold this season. It's like they're reminding us—it's still their land."

Miakoda leaned forward, her eyes deep with meaning.

"The wolves," she said softly, "are more than flesh and fur. They are spirits, Sheridan. Messengers. They move in time with the moon—my namesake—and speak in a language older than any of ours. Their presence means something. They ask us to remember our place."

He nodded, taking in her words.

She went on. "They teach unity. Resilience. They survive by relying on each other. They don't ask for power—they carry it. Their bond with the moon is not just myth. It's rhythm. Cycle. Reminder."

Ahanu's voice followed hers, low and firm.

"They've always been with us. Same as the rivers. Same as the wind. Watching them teaches you how to live right. We walk here because they let us. We remember that."

Their words hung in the air—not heavy, but full. He sat with them, letting the silence stretch. The crackle of fire. The echo of footsteps beyond the door.

The conversation turned to other things—ways of knowing, ways of seeing. Of living within, not on top of, the land. Theirs was a knowledge drawn from generations. Not written. Lived.

And for a while, under that roof, in the company of those who understood the language of the wild better than most, he felt something shift in him.

Not a change.

A return.

As dusk deepened and the feast neared, stories unfurled like smoke, and laughter rose warm into the rafters. He sat among them—not apart, not other. Just present. And grateful.

30

He woke to a world freshly cloaked in snow, the white expanse softening every edge of the settlement. The silence it brought was thick, reverent. The kind that made sound feel like intrusion. Cold reached into his bones, convincing him to linger beneath the warmth of his blankets. No fire, no coffee yet. Just stillness.

Then came a knock—a gentle rapping at the door. Miakoda, knowing his rhythms better than most, stepped in with a gift: a steaming cup of coffee. Its aroma curled into the room, earthy and familiar. He accepted it without words, the heat seeping into his fingers, then deeper.

She placed a bowl beside him next—a rich venison stew, thick with parsnip and carrot, the broth spiced and slow-cooked. Beside it, the bannock still warm from the fire, perfect for soaking up the last of the broth.

"It's good to have you here," she said softly, setting the bread within reach.

He met her gaze, gratitude settling in his chest. "And good to be here. You've outdone yourself, Miakoda."

She gave a small, knowing smile. "It's just stew. But it travels well—straight to the heart."

They shared no more words, none needed. He ate slowly, savoring each bite as if it contained the settlement's spirit. The warmth of the food stayed with him long after the bowl was empty.

Outside, the hush of snow blanketed the world. The trees, their limbs heavy with white, leaned into the silence. He adjusted his scarf, checked his pack, and stepped into the morning.

Ahanu joined him there, breath visible in the crisp air. He handed him a small pouch—dried meats and herbs wrapped in cloth.

"For the journey," he said.

He met his eyes. "Staying with you, sharing in your lives, even just for a while—it's meant more than I can say. The warmth of your fire. The wisdom in your words. Thank you."

Ahanu clasped his hand, firm and steady. "You're always welcome here. The land knows you, Sheridan. And so do we. Travel safe."

Miakoda added, "The land watches over those who walk gently. May the forest guide your steps. And when you return, there'll be stories and fire waiting."

He nodded, their words settling in his chest like coals.

"I'm heading to Keg River. If you need anything from Frank Jackson or the trading post, I'll take it."

Ahanu's eyes lit with the offer. "We'll put together a few items for trade. Thank you, my friend."

With farewells exchanged, pouch tucked into his pack, he turned toward the trail.

Two inches of fresh snow muted the world. Each step pressed gently into the white, his boots leaving a slow, deliberate record of passage. The forest whispered around him, branches creaking, a jay calling once from deep within. The world had exhaled.

Four hours later, he crested the ridge.

The shack waited—a modest silhouette above the Peace River valley. Below, the world spread out in stillness. Elk would come. They always did, drawn by the quiet current of migration that moved through this place like breath.

The shack was simple. A stove. A cot. A view. But it was the meat cache that marked this place as sacred.

Ten years ago, he had built it—an underground chamber lined with stone and cedar, insulated with soil and bark, tucked beneath the frost line. It was never meant for permanence. Just enough time to prepare. Just enough time to move without waste.

The cache was a compromise with the wild—a place to keep what he harvested before the bears or the cold could claim it. Practical, but more than that. It spoke of knowledge passed down, of lives lived close to need. Of not taking more than you could carry.

Inside, he lit the stove. Flames caught, casting long shadows that danced along the walls. The warmth grew slow and honest.

He unpacked in silence. Hung his coat. Checked the hinges. The place had held.

Outside, the wind moved through the trees, slow and sure. Tomorrow, he'd scout the migration path. Maybe lay a trap. Maybe not.

For now, he stood at the window, the valley below veiled in stillness. It wasn't loneliness he felt—it was the fullness of solitude. The weight of being exactly where he was meant to be.

He thought of Miakoda's words—*'the land watching those who walk gently'*. Of Ahanu's grip, strong and steady. And further back, of his wife's laugh echoing across the cabin walls, of his daughter's first snow angel carved into the ground outside their old home. Memory came not in a rush, but like a snowfall— silent, sure, covering everything in its own time.

The forest did not speak. But he listened just the same.

31

Snow fell through the trees in wide, slow spirals. By morning, five inches had settled, blanketing the trapline, softening the contours of the land. Sheridan rose early, his breath forming ghosts in the air. Today, he would repair the old pitfall.

The work was hard and silent. The kind that tethered a man to the earth. He cleared the snow first, revealing the old scar in the ground, then began reshaping it—deepening, widening, reinforcing its walls with planks he cut and hauled himself. It sat along an ancient elk path, one he had mapped in his bones over decades. The pit, camouflaged with snow-dusted branches and debris, became invisible again—dangerous, but necessary.

He lined the bottom with leaves. Not for comfort, exactly. But out of respect.

By dusk, wind picked up, a hard cold threading through the trees. He retreated to the shack.

Inside, the stove flickered to life, casting amber warmth across the room. He moved slowly, hands red from cold, joints aching. He lit the lantern, hung his coat, then sat.

In the quiet, he began preparing snares. Wire, bent and shaped with care. His fingers moved instinctively, his mind elsewhere—drifting toward Miakoda's soft smile, Ahanu's voice by the fire. He thought of his wife —how she'd laugh at him fussing over these wires like he was braiding hair. Her voice came unbidden, warm in his mind.

The snares formed a tidy pile. Each one a whisper of purpose. A promise.

That night, the forest outside was restless. A distant howl stitched its way across the darkness. He sat for a long time, fire crackling low, listening. Then sleep took him, slow and sure.

He woke to a world remade. A foot of snow. Trees heavy with white. The air held that deep, undisturbed stillness only winter could summon. He laced his boots, strapped on his father's snowshoes, and stepped out.

The descent from the hilltop shack was deliberate. Each step pressing a memory into the snow. Chickadees chattered in the branches. A hare bounded across his path, its coat almost invisible. Fox tracks looped through the underbrush. Life endured, even here.

At the river's edge, he paused. The Peace ran beneath a thin veneer of ice, its breath audible in the hush. He uncovered his canoe, buried beneath brush, and made a small fire with his spirit stove. Coffee, smoked meat, a wedge of hard cheese. A ritual.

Then came the ice.

With a branch, he broke through the rim at the riverbank. Shards scattered, the sound sharp against silence. He worked slowly, patiently, until the canoe could pass. The act was physical, immediate. A man versus winter, not in conquest, but in understanding.

Once the canoe slipped free, he pushed off, paddling hard into the current. Behind him, the shore fell away.

The river held him.

Halfway across, he paused. The vastness of it all—the sky, the snow, the dark line of trees stretching like a memory across the horizon. He was small here. But he was known.

Carcajou rose ahead, tucked in the trees. As he crested the last hill, the cabin came into view—smoke curling from the chimney in a thin, steady line.
His pulse quickened.
He hadn't expected visitors.

The hike up from the river had been quiet. No signs,

no voices. But now, as he stepped off the trail and into the clearing, unease settled in his chest.

Snow covered the clearing in a soft, deceptive hush. But the surface was broken—footprints, several sets, tracked in every direction.

Not just one person. And not just passing through.

The tracks fanned out around the cabin like something had been searched for. The snow near the root cellar was trampled, churned. A second set of tracks looped toward the woodshed, then back. Another set circled the cabin twice before disappearing out of view.

Too many for comfort. Too restless for hunters.

He moved slowly, crouching near the treeline, eyes fixed on the door. The windows gave nothing away— curtains drawn. No shadows moved behind the glass.

He waited, breath low. One hand rested on the haft of his knife. The other, still gloved, gripped the snow-packed earth.

Who had come? And why?

The wilderness taught many lessons. One of them was this: when the land is too quiet, something is wrong.

DJ ATKINSON

PART 3

DJ ATKINSON

32

In the hush of a snow-draped morning, Sheridan approached his cabin in Carcajou with the cautious gait of a man long-acquainted with the wild's unpredictable temperament. A fresh foot of snow softened the world to silence, muffling his footsteps as he neared the familiar outline of the cabin —a structure that had weathered more than storms.

He paused just short of the porch. The snow around the doorway was marred by several sets of prints, scuffed and backtracked, as if those who made them had loitered or reconsidered their steps. Something tightened in his chest. With a slow breath, he laid a gloved hand on the latch and pushed the door inward.

Warmth met him, but not the kind he was used to. The air inside was heavy, touched with the scent of damp wool and bodies that didn't belong. Four men turned as one. None smiled.

At the forefront stood a man whose posture spoke for the rest. Samuel. Broad-shouldered, eyes cool and measuring, he stepped forward—not reaching for a weapon, but with a stillness that implied one might not be far. "Who're you, then?" he asked, the edge in his tone dull, but unmistakable.

He kept his hands visible as he stepped fully inside, snow melting in clumps around his boots. "Name's Sheridan," he said evenly. "This cabin's mine. Wasn't expecting company."

A moment's beat passed, taut with uncertainty.

William stood up beside Samuel. "We're just passing through," he offered, his voice smoother, more deliberate. "Weather caught us. Didn't mean to trespass."

James and Ethan watched from behind, silent and taut, like hounds waiting on signal. Their expressions were unreadable, though something behind their eyes sparked—relief, perhaps, that Sheridan wasn't shouting, or shooting.

"Well," he said, scanning the space as if to confirm his own memories of it, "you've found a solid roof. You're welcome to the warmth." He glanced toward the stove. "Storm's not letting up anytime soon. Planning to move on?"

Samuel exchanged a look with William, unreadable. "Eventually," he answered. Then, a beat later, James added, "If that's alright with you, Sheridan." It came out tentative, the first olive branch—an attempt to placate, to gauge his temper.

"Long as you're not tearing the place apart," he replied, his tone mild. "This cabin's stood a long time. I'd like it to see a while longer."

Silence returned, broken only by the crackle of the stove. He stepped farther into the room. His gaze swept over the blankets, gear stacked in corners, his belongings displaced. He made no move to shed his coat.

He moved to the counter and set down his pack. Then, with practiced routine, began making himself a mug of coffee—boiling water, measuring grounds from a jar that looked a third lighter than it should have. As the scent rose, rich and bitter, he turned.

"Noticed a fair bit of my stores are gone."

There was a shift in the air. William straightened. "We've eaten what we needed."

Then, with a dry smirk, he reached into his coat pocket and drew out a small fold of American bills. He tossed them onto the table. "This should cover it."

The gesture was too casual, too rehearsed. He stared at the money, then at the man who had tossed it.

"Strange currency for this far north," he said quietly.

William lifted his shoulders in a shrug, "Money

spends the same, no matter how far north you are."

He sipped his coffee. The mug warmed his hands, but his eyes remained cool. He pulled a chair from the wall, dragging it into a corner of the room. Not quite a barrier, not quite an invitation.

He began sorting through his gear. Reclaiming space. Occupying silence.

The men talked in low murmurs, trading looks, watching him out of the corners of their eyes.

They sat with the fire between them, but the chill was elsewhere. He reached into his pack, pulled free a piece of bannock and some jerky, and tore a corner off. A slow chew, a wash of coffee from his tin cup. He made no offer to share. Not out of cruelty—Just clarity.

He let the quiet stretch. Then, with a casual tone that didn't match the sharpness in his gaze, he said, "This cabin's been shelter for all kinds over the years. Plenty of stories told by that stove."

William's gaze flicked to the bannock, then away. "We're just grateful for the shelter," he said, voice flat. No story offered. No name given.

He gave a slow nod, as though weighing the temperature of something more than the coffee.

The night pressed in. Wind hissed softly at the corners of the cabin, and the fire gave off more light than heat. They sat like men at a card table, each holding something close.

He didn't know what they were hiding—but he knew it wasn't just cold or hunger.

And William, watching Sheridan from across the room, knew the old man wasn't fooled.

Tomorrow, the snow might lift—but it wouldn't be the first thing to crack.

The first light of dawn seeped into the cabin, casting a soft glow on the makeshift sleeping arrangements. Sheridan, having claimed his bed back the night before—a silent declaration of his authority—rose with the sun, his movements deliberate in the quiet of the early morning.

The rustle of blankets and the soft groans of waking men filled the space as he went about his morning routine, the clink of his coffee pot a stark contrast to the silence that had enveloped the cabin overnight. Samuel watched him with a steely gaze from his spot on the floor, the unspoken tension between them lingering like the chill in the air.

"Morning," he offered, his voice breaking the stillness, carrying a note of civility that belied the underlying discomfort of their situation. "Planning on heading to Keg River soon. You mentioned you were going that way?"

William sat up, rubbing the sleep from his eyes, his wariness mirrored in the quick glances exchanged with his companions. "Yeah, we did say that," he replied cautiously, "but with the weather clearing up, we might hold off a bit longer. Got some... planning to do."

Pouring his coffee, he nodded as if he hadn't expected any other answer. "Suit yourselves. The offer stands if you change your mind. Road to Keg River can be tricky this time of year," he said, a subtle reminder of the dangers that lay outside the cabin's walls. Samuel finally spoke up, his voice gruff with sleep and suspicion. "We appreciate it, but we'll manage. You seem in a hurry to get there yourself."

Leaning against the counter with his coffee in hand, he met his gaze. "Just things to take care of, like anyone else. Besides, the cabin's getting a bit crowded, don't you think?"

The comment hung in the air, a light jest tinged with truth. The men, sensing the undercurrent of his words, exchanged uneasy looks. His insistence on Keg River, coupled with his nonchalance, did little to ease William's growing suspicion that he might know more than he let on.

As the men began to stir more fully, the cabin buzzed with the energy of the day beginning. Finishing his coffee, he started to gather his things, his movements signaling his readiness to depart.

William watched him, a plan forming in his mind. Once he was gone, they would need to make their move quickly. The cabin, a temporary haven, was no longer safe, not with the possibility of his return or, worse, him bringing back others from Keg River. "We'll see you off, then," William said, standing. "Safe travels to Keg River."

Pausing at the door, he looked back at the men. "Take care of the place," he said, a parting reminder of the cabin's significance, not just as a shelter, but as a home within the wild.

With that, he stepped out into the morning light, leaving behind the cabin and the men whose secrets lay as hidden and deep as the snow that blanketed the ground outside. The silence of his departure was a relief to William, but it was also a countdown to their imminent departure, a race against time and suspicion in the unforgiving wilderness.

He set out from the cabin with a palpable sense of urgency propelling him forward, his snowshoes cutting a determined path through the fresh snow. The morning air was crisp, the sky a clear expanse of blue that promised a day of favorable weather for his journey to Keg River. As he navigated the familiar terrain, the rhythm of his movement allowed his thoughts to drift, reflecting on the encounter with the strangers in his cabin.

He couldn't shake the feeling that he had just skirted the edge of a potentially dangerous situation. The tension in the cabin, the guarded looks exchanged among the men, and their vague answers to his questions had set off alarm bells in his mind. He couldn't shake the sense he'd just shared a roof with something far worse than bad weather. He considered the possibility that his departure, timed as it was with the break of dawn, might have been the safest move. It wasn't just the need to reach Keg River that hastened his steps but an instinctual drive to put distance between himself and whatever the men were planning.

He pushed himself, aiming to complete the journey in under nine hours—a testament to his resilience and the urgency driving him. The landscape around him, usually a source of solace and connection, now served as a stark backdrop to his contemplations.

Despite the beauty of the day, his mind was preoccupied with the recent events. *'Did William catch on to my suspicions?'* He wondered, replaying their final exchange in his mind. The subtle dance of words and looks had been fraught with unspoken tension, a mutual recognition of something left unsaid. He considered the possibility that his own guarded responses and pointed questions might have revealed more than he intended, perhaps alerting William to his wariness.

Keg River drew nearer, his determination solidified. The journey had not just been a physical test but a mental one, a period of introspection and decision-making. He acknowledged the relief he felt at having left the cabin when he did, trusting his instincts over the comfort of ignorance. The thought of alerting the authorities or seeking help in Keg River crossed his mind, a consideration he would need to approach with care.

As his figure merged with the treeline, vanishing into the dense woods, William stood by the cabin window, a silent sentinel pondering the ramifications of their latest encounter. The departure of Sheridan, with his calm demeanor and probing questions, left a tangible unease in the air. He was no stranger to suspicion, and the way he had carried himself, the subtle authority with which he reclaimed his space, hinted at a man not easily fooled. *'Did he know? Could he have guessed who we are?'* he mused, his mind turning over possibilities like stones in a stream.

Inside the cabin, the atmosphere shifted from watchful tension to focused strategy. Samuel began checking gear with methodical precision, laying out packs and counting rations. Ethan paced slowly, not with panic, but with thought. James leaned against the wall near the stove, arms crossed, considering the landscape in his head.

James was first to speak, voice pitched high with worry. "We need to move. Now. If he figures it out—"

Ethan paced. "What if he already has? What if he's going for help?"

Samuel stood slowly, his expression unreadable. "We're not running from some old trapper." But even his voice had lost its edge.

He spoke last, decisive. "We leave at dawn. Not west—not where he's headed. East, then north. It'll slow any pursuit."

James bristled. "We've burned through most of the food."

"Take what's left," he said. "He didn't leave us stocked, and he won't be back with gifts."

Ethan hesitated. "Should we have... dealt with him?"

He turned, eyes cold. "No. Killing him would've lit a beacon. Right now, they don't know who we are. That's our edge."

They gathered their things with quiet purpose, the weight of decision heavy but not frantic. They tightened straps, coiled rope and folded maps. Outside, the day was clear. The snow held no footprints but Sheridan's.

William felt the shift. Sheridan had changed something. The old man hadn't pushed. But he'd seen too much.

Night settled slow and sure. They spoke little. The stove snapped softly. The cabin, once a haven, now felt like borrowed time.

Outside, the wilderness waited. And somewhere out there, he moved with purpose—toward help, toward warning, toward whatever storm lay ahead.

33

Sheridan pushed open the door to the trading post, his steps sluggish, wearied from the long trek through snow and solitude. The warm interior hit him like a wall—woodsmoke, cured leather, and the faint scent of dried herbs. At the counter, Frank Jackson looked up from his ledger, his face breaking into surprise and welcome.

"Sheridan! By all that's holy—I wasn't expecting you until the thaw. What brings you through so early?"

He managed a tired smile, shaking snow from his coat. "It feels like I've been wrestling bears just to get here."

Frank rounded the counter, grasping his friend's hand firmly. "Well, bears or not, you look half frozen. Come on, you're staying the night. No arguments. There's stew on the stove, and you're due a proper rest."

He nodded, too hollowed out by cold and distance to argue. "That sounds about perfect. I've got a story to tell, Frank. One I can barely believe myself."

Frank led him toward the back rooms, where heat from the woodstove thickened the air and the light took on a golden hue. In the small kitchen, he sat heavily while Frank ladled out bowls of hearty stew, the kind built on winter root vegetables and memory.

They ate in companionable silence at first. Then Sheridan began to speak.

He described the four men, how they'd arrived with the storm, their evasive answers, the tension that hummed beneath every word they spoke. Frank's expression darkened with each detail.

"Four of them?" he asked, setting his spoon down slowly. "You know, that might not be random. There've been break-ins around Keg River. Cabins hit for supplies. People saw four strangers... moving fast."

He stood, walked over to the cluttered corkboard near the back pantry. He returned with a folded sheet of paper and laid it flat on the table. A wanted poster. Four faces.

"These the men?"

Sheridan leaned in. Recognition hit like a punch to the chest. "That's them. William. Samuel. James. Ethan."

Frank leaned back in his chair, his expression folding

into something between disbelief and grief. "They're wanted for murder. Butte, Montana. U.S. Marshals tipped off the RCMP weeks ago. Word is they crossed the border and vanished."

Silence fell again, heavier now.

Sheridan exhaled slowly. "They said the storm trapped them. That they were passing through. I offered shelter. If I'd known—"

Frank shook his head. "You did what any man would've. But now we know. We have to act. We go to the RCMP first thing tomorrow."

Sheridan nodded, jaw set. "I'll tell them everything."

The rest of the evening passed in low conversation, the mood subdued but focused. The comfort of the trading post had become a war room. Tomorrow, their course would change.

The next morning dawned bitter and bright. Frank already had coffee on when Sheridan entered the kitchen, the air thick with roasted warmth and urgency.

They sat hunched over a map. Sheridan traced trails with his fingertip, as if drawing lines through snow he hadn't yet crossed.

"If they bolt, they'll head west. Fastest route through the trees. If we take the ridge trail, we can get a view of the cabin before they know we're coming."

Frank nodded. "But we need backup. McFee's the only one close enough. I'll ride."

"Be careful," Sheridan said. "Tell him everything. We can't afford missteps."

Frank saddled a sturdy bay and vanished into the white. The day passed in a slow grind, tension mounting with each hour.

By dusk, he returned, wind bitten and breathless, but not alone. Mountie Tim McFee followed, tall in his saddle, uniform crisp despite the ride. He dismounted, nodded once.

"Morning," he said the next day as they gathered at the table. He unrolled his own map. "We approach from the rear slope. Sheridan, you're our guide. Frank, you'll cover the flank. We stay low. No engagement unless absolutely necessary."

Sheridan nodded, the weight of it anchoring somewhere between his ribs. He'd welcomed strangers with the best part of himself—his trust. And now he had to become something else entirely.

McFee's eyes swept over them both. "These men are desperate. Desperate men do foolish things. But remember—they're still men. This isn't just a matter of justice. It's about how we carry it out."

None of them spoke after that for a long time.

Outside, the sky turned from iron to silver.

Snowflakes began to fall—slow, patient, and knowing. Sheridan pulled on his coat. Whatever peace he'd known had been traded for something heavier. Something necessary.

The cabin in the hills waited. And so did the reckoning.

34

The trek to his cabin was charged with a mix of anticipation and unease. Snow whispered beneath their boots, crisp and untouched, the trees holding their breath beneath a leaden sky. The air cut sharp against their faces, and the silence—vast and listening—settled over them like a held breath.

Sheridan, leading with the surety of someone who knew every shadow and rise of this land, halted at the edge of the clearing. The cabin stood motionless among the drifts, half-buried, its chimney cold. He stared at it a moment longer than necessary.

"No smoke," he murmured. "They've gone."

Frank stepped beside him, tightening his coat with a gloved hand. "Maybe they saw us coming. Made a run for it."

McFee shook his head, eyes narrowing. "No rush in the

tracks. No panic. They left on their own terms—and not recently."

They stepped inside. The cold met them like an accusation. The stove sat lifeless, a dusting of ash on the iron. Sheridan scanned the interior, the familiar space now hollowed and violated.

"They took what they could carry," he said. "Blankets, stores... my father's old rifle."

McFee crouched at the door. "Tracks lead toward the river. Let's move."

They followed the narrow path through the woods, boots cracking through crusted snow, branches whispering above. At the river's edge, McFee motioned them over.

The tracks descended to the frozen channel in a quiet arc, deliberate and unhurried. Across the water, Sheridan's canoe sat marooned on the far side, gleaming with ice, its stillness almost accusatory.

"They crossed," McFee said. "Left the canoe. They're on foot now."

Sheridan's jaw tightened. "They'll keep moving until the trees swallow them. We wait—we lose them."

McFee's gaze lingered on the opposite shore, calculating. "We don't know their route. Charging in would be guesswork. We need more men. We regroup. We'll find them."

Frank nodded, reluctantly. "I'll head back. Raise the alarm. Supplies, men. We'll be ready next time."

Sheridan stood still, his eyes on the river. "I'm staying."

Frank turned, surprised. "Here? Alone?"

"This is my home," he said. "I need to put it right. I'll get word to my family. Let them know I'm safe."

McFee gripped his reins. "Take care, Sheridan. We'll be back soon."

Sheridan watched them ride out, the snow swallowing hoofbeats and bootprints alike. The cabin behind him stood empty. The silence it offered felt different now—less like peace, more like waiting.

Inside, shadows leaned across the floor, stretching long in the fading light. The stolen warmth, the missing rifle, the absence of voices—it all hung in the air like smoke that refused to clear.

His mind turned to Ahanu.

Friend, neighbor, more than either word could capture. Ahanu had steadied him through seasons both harsh and kind. He remembered the quiet strength of his friend's voice, the way he once built a fire that saved them both in a blizzard. He owed him more than words. The thought of those men —armed, cornered, dangerous—stumbling toward Ahanu's homestead burned in his chest.

He sat briefly, then stood.

Waiting wasn't enough. Not with the trail cooling and the stakes rising.

They were doing what they could. But he knew the land. He could move through it quieter, faster. He could cut them off.

He rolled a blanket, packed salt meat and a flask of tea. Checked his boots, cinched his coat.

'I'll move along the river,' he thought. 'Stay to the trees. If I'm right, I'll see their fire before they ever see mine.'

He paused before leaving, hand resting where his father's rifle once hung. A different kind of weapon would guide him now.

With one last glance at the cabin—this wounded place that had been his home—he stepped into the dusk.

The trail ahead was uncertain, but the wild had always spoken to him in ways no map ever could.

35

They reached the Peace River by dusk, wind sighing low through the trees. Sheridan's canoe waited on the near bank, caught in a lattice of ice and drift.

"We're crossing," William said, scanning the far shore. "Put distance between us and Keg River."

James hesitated, eyeing the vessel. "That thing? I'll end up swimming."

"You'll stay dry if you don't panic," William muttered, already positioning the canoe. "Ethan, James—you're first."

Samuel's voice, low and sharp, sliced through the air. "We're not arguing. Get in."

The river greeted them with teeth. As Ethan took the stern and James the bow, the current dragged at them like something alive. The canoe rocked and groaned.

Water slapped the sides.

"Steady," Ethan snapped, voice tight. "Don't fight it. Just match me."

James gritted his teeth, paddle jerking through the current. "I am! The damn boat's the problem."

They hit a shelf of slush, and the canoe pitched violently. James yelped.

"Breathe! You panic, we both go in," Ethan growled, adjusting their course with a sharp pivot.

By the time they scraped ashore, breathless and shaking, neither spoke. Ethan's knuckles were white on the gunwale.

"That was too close," he muttered.

He turned, breath misting, and forced himself back into the canoe. The second crossing waited.

Samuel watched from the bank, a cigarette burning slow in his hand. When Ethan arrived, he climbed in with wordless resolve.

"You sure?" Ethan asked, but it wasn't really a question.

Samuel nodded once. He didn't deal in fear—not the kind you could see.

The current was no gentler. They paddled in silence, Samuel's strokes precise, metered. Ethan's arms ached, but he didn't complain.

"How do you stay calm?" he asked.

Samuel kept his gaze forward. "Because fear won't get us across. Action will."

The canoe bumped into snow-packed earth, and Samuel stepped out, shaking off the cold like a dog. He didn't speak, just lit another cigarette and nodded toward the river.

"Last trip," he said, already climbing back in.

James and Ethan crouched low in the brush, steam rising from their wet clothes. James rubbed his arms.

"This place hates people," he muttered.

Ethan gave a dry laugh. "You think Samuel's even human?"

James snorted. "And William—if he tells us to keep moving one more time..."

But there was no real venom in it. Only weariness.

Ethan leaned back against a tree. "Still. We made it. That counts."

James nodded slowly. "Yeah. Just doesn't feel like a win. Not yet."

The silence returned, vast and indifferent. In it, something like solidarity began to settle.

When William and Samuel took the final crossing, the river held its breath. Alone in the boat, the tension loosened. No need for show. Just truth.

William's voice broke the hush. "You ever think we'd be better off without them? Just you and me?"

Samuel didn't turn. "All the time. Doesn't mean it's true."

William exhaled, watching mist form and vanish. "Ethan panicked. James complains like it's his job."

"And you didn't? Back in Calgary? First run we ever made? You shook so bad I thought you'd drop the keys."

William grunted. "That was different."

"Sure it was."

They paddled a while longer.

Samuel added, more gently, "People harden in the fire. Some melt, some forge. We're about to find out which is which."

The far shore rose up before them. William nodded. "You're right. I just... this land doesn't forgive mistakes."

Samuel's voice was steady. "Then we don't make any. Not the kind we can't fix."

The canoe kissed earth. Samuel stepped out, reached a hand to steady the bow. William climbed out, jaw tight.

For a long moment, they stood in the snow, breath

clouding. The river behind them stilled.

"We'll make it," William said.

Samuel lit a cigarette. The flare of the match was brief.

"Yup."

And that was enough.

They veered south along the shoreline, hoping for easier ground. But the terrain betrayed them. Snowdrifts hid slick stones; ice sheared off beneath their weight. Wind scraped at their faces like claws.

"Watch your step," William called, voice barely cresting the roar of the river. "The ice is bad."

James slipped first. One foot plunged into the river, water biting up his leg. "Damn it! Not again," he cursed, dragging himself back onto the bank, soaked and shivering. "Montana's cold, but this? This is hell dressed in white."

No one laughed.

Ethan cursed as he lost footing on a slope glazed in frost. He caught himself with a groan. "We're not built for this," he muttered, breath clouding in bursts.

William stopped. Snow gathered on his shoulders, unshaken. "This is no good. Inland. Now."

No one questioned him. Not anymore.

The shift was instinctual. Into the woods, away from the river's edge. Trees rose around them, closing ranks. Snow muffled their passage, save for the crunch of boots and the occasional ragged breath.

They found the footprints at the base of a slope—sharp, fresh, unmistakable.

"Someone's ahead," William said, crouching. The prints fanned east, ascending.

James leaned in, hope flickering behind his fatigue. "Finally, something going our way."

Ethan shot him a look. "Or leading us into a trap."

Samuel knelt, palm brushing the print. "They're recent. They might have shelter. Or fire. Either way—we follow."

Their pace quickened. The forest narrowed as the incline steepened. Snow clung to every branch, heavy as silence. The climb tested them. James slipped again. Swore. Fell.

"This hill's cursed," he spat.

Samuel offered no sympathy. "Watch where you put your feet."

Ethan chuckled until he, too, nearly tumbled. "Climbing a waterfall of snow," he gasped.

At last, the ridge broke. Trees thinned. And there—crouched like a secret kept too long—stood a shack.

They didn't speak. Just moved.

Samuel led them to the door. The shack was spartan,

weather-beaten, angled into the wind. It offered no promise, only walls. But it was enough.

Inside, the cold was absolute, dense as stone. Still, it was shelter.

"Stove," Samuel barked. "James."

James moved fast, grateful for instruction.

"Ethan, food. Whatever's here."

Ethan scoured the cupboards, muttering. "Sure. Make me the scavenger. Again."

William lingered at the door, eyes tracing the line of the valley below. Peace River, silvered and distant, flowed like a blade through the wilderness.

Then a voice: "Hey. Look at this."

Ethan held up a knife, wooden-handled, etched with a name. *Sheridan.*

William stepped forward, took it. His expression shifted—recognition, then something darker. "This is his."

The shack stilled around them.

James was first to break it. "We're in his place? Sheridan's? The guy who's probably hunting us now?"

Ethan gave a dry laugh. "Well. That's rich."

Samuel leaned into the wall, cigarette flaring. "Then we're not just trespassers. We're fools. He knows this terrain. This place. We're exposed."

William nodded slowly, setting the knife on the table. "We move at first light. No noise. Just rest, and watch."

Still, James lit the stove. Hunger and cold were louder than fear.

Later, Ethan stepped out into the dark, fumbling with his coat. Snowflakes settled silently as he wandered from the door.

A snap, sharp and metallic.

His scream ripped through the silence. "Damn it!"

Samuel emerged, unhurried. He lit a cigarette before even looking.

Ethan thrashed in a snare, one leg caught in a wire loop, pain drawn across his face like frostbite.

Samuel smirked. "The land doesn't care if you're pissing or praying. It'll catch you either way."

He winced. "This isn't funny. Help me out."

"Lesson's worth more when it stings," Samuel said, then sighed. "Hold still."

The snare yielded. Ethan collapsed to one knee.

"Try to piss before dark next time," Samuel muttered, hauling him up.

Inside, laughter flickered like firelight—sharp, brief, uneasy.

Night settled.

William remained by the window, watching shadows stretch across snow. He felt the edges of exhaustion, but sleep stayed distant. The warmth from the stove couldn't thaw what lay ahead.

They'd escaped across the river. Climbed into wilderness. Found momentary shelter. But everything—every step, every warmth—came with a cost.

Tomorrow, the cold would return. And so would the hunt.

36

Sheridan dragged the spare canoe down from the cabin—one normally reserved for family excursions. It scraped across the snow like a memory being pulled from deep beneath the surface. The sun had long tilted west by the time he launched into the Peace River, arms burning from the weight of both effort and urgency. Each stroke bit into the current. Each breath came sharp.

He landed beside the other canoe—abandoned, half-frozen into the bank. It confirmed what the snow already said: the men had crossed here. Fresh tracks climbed the hill. Staggered, deep-set tracks spoke of exhaustion, haste, and no plan beyond escape.

He followed.

The climb bent his lungs and tightened his jaw. Halfway up, he paused behind a stand of spruce, crouching low to scan the terrain. His cabin sat quiet on the ridge, dark and unguarded. Smokeless chimney. No prints circling the threshold. Still, he waited, eyes locked on the door.

Then he moved.

Inside, the cold was invasive. His home lay gutted—rations stripped, gear scattered, the cot upturned. The stove door hung ajar. Nothing stolen with precision, only grabbed. Violated.

Outside, a snare lay tripped and tangled. Blood in the snow. Briefly caught, and gone.

He lit the stove. Warmth crawled back into the corners of the shack. But his thoughts were already elsewhere—at the settlement, at Ahanu's family. If the fugitives kept moving east, they might stumble upon it. Desperate men with nothing left often took everything from those who did.

He sat through the dark with the fire low and a rifle across his knees. Sleep flirted but never stayed.

At first light, Sheridan packed. A canvas roll of dried meat. The rifle. A pouch of bullets. Then he locked the cabin, as if it still held something sacred. As if the land hadn't already been breached.

By midmorning, he'd reached the high ridge above the settlement. A hawk wheeled overhead. The snow gave no fresh signs—nothing ahead of him but old prospector paths winding through the hills like veins of a forgotten era.

He took the steep descent eastward. Ahanu's settlement shimmered into view, its edges softened by the mist that rose from morning fires. And then —familiar steps approaching. Ahanu's form emerged from the trees, steady and grounded.

"Sheridan," he called. No alarm, but no ease either.

"You're safe," Sheridan exhaled. "That's something."

Ahanu nodded toward the cabin. "Come inside. You look like the land has been speaking to you."

Miakoda met them at the door, offering coffee without a word. She saw it in Sheridan's posture—the way a man sits when his news is heavier than his pack.

"Close to dawn," he said, answering her unspoken question. "They've been through my place. Took what they could. Left it hollow."

Ahanu's face tensed, then steadied. "Did they follow the trail here?"

"No. That's the strange part. They veered east, away from the river path. Took the prospector's route instead."

"I saw them," Ahanu said. "At a distance. Arguing. They don't know where they're going."

Miakoda's voice was a hush. "Fugitives? Armed?"

Sheridan gave a slow nod. "And scared. Which makes them dangerous."

The silence between them held the shape of possibility. Sheridan broke it.

"I came to warn you. You, the families here... they're not ready for what's out there."

Ahanu turned to Miakoda. "That's why I didn't tell you."

Her gaze met his. No anger—just understanding. "You trust the land. So do I."

She reached for Sheridan's hand. "And we trust you. But we won't sleep through this."

Ahanu's voice was calm. "The land will test them. It teaches hard lessons. If they try to take from it, it will answer."

Sheridan stood. "Still. I need to keep moving. My family's not far. And if these men reach them..."

Ahanu rose with him. "Then we'll stand ready."

Miakoda offered a final word. "We don't live in fear. But we do listen. And the land is speaking."

Sheridan left with that voice in his bones. The path ahead was uncertain, but no longer alone. The land was not just terrain. It was a witness, and it would not be kind to those who trespassed blind.

The snow held his tracks for a while. Then, like memory, they softened and disappeared.

37

The morning broke brittle and pale. Frost veiled the earth in silence as William studied the diverging trails ahead. Behind him, the others shifted restlessly, a low tension crackling beneath their stillness like ice underfoot.

"I'm not going anywhere near that damn river again," James muttered, his voice sharp with memory. "Higher ground. Drier. Safer."

Ethan leaned into the weight of his bruised leg and nodded, jaw tight. "It's stable enough. I'm not risking another fall."

Samuel stood apart, cigarette glowing faintly in the blue-tinged cold. Smoke curled around his face, hiding nothing. His breath rose in clouds, but his eyes remained fixed on the horizon—distant, impassive.

James and Ethan hunched together beneath stolen

blankets, their complaints whispering through clenched teeth. "Blankets. That's it? We'll freeze before midnight," James muttered. Ethan shifted, his discomfort more raw than angry.

Samuel let the silence stretch, then exhaled. "Pick a direction. We need shelter before nightfall."

William motioned toward the slope. "The hillside path. Less risk of being swept under again."

Samuel dropped the cigarette, crushing it under his boot. The ember hissed and vanished.

They moved.

The trail wound through thin timber and brush-buried stone. Footing was uncertain, each step a test of will. The cold pressed in from all sides, not as a storm but a slow, patient suffocation.

Ethan's leg slowed him. James muttered, half-hearted defiance stripped of conviction. The grumbling rose until Samuel stopped.

He turned, abrupt.

"Enough."

The word landed hard. James blinked. Ethan froze.

Samuel's voice dropped, colder than the air. "You think I enjoy this? Think this is some goddamn wilderness retreat? We're not tourists. We're not safe. We're hunted. You want to keep whining? Or do you want to survive?"

They walked on. This time, in silence. William let it hang. He didn't need to add to it.

Eventually, James looked down. Ethan said nothing.

William's voice came quiet. "We get through tonight. Then we talk."

They found a shallow hollow against a granite outcrop. It wasn't much, but it offered a break from the wind. Samuel dropped his bundle, eyes scanning for firewood.

"James. Fire. Ethan, help him!"

The men scattered. Snow covered most of what was usable, but they gathered what they could—twigs, pine needles, bark ripped from dead limbs. James struck match after match, each one fading into smoke.

"Keep at it," William said. Calm. Unflinching.

Finally, a spark caught. The flame stuttered, then held. Ethan returned, dropping frozen wood beside it. Together, they coaxed it into a glow.

Night descended with no ceremony. Wolves howled from somewhere beyond the reach of firelight—long, low calls that braided into the cold.

James stiffened. "That's close."

"Great," Ethan muttered. "Freezing wasn't enough."

Samuel didn't look up. "They're watching. That's all." He took a long drag. "They're smart enough to stay back—unless we give them reason."

William added, "Keep the fire strong. Make noise if they approach. They're opportunists, not soldiers."

They nodded. The fire became their shield, their fragile center in the vastness. James fed it in silence. Ethan hovered near, limping less from pain than from fear.

Samuel flicked his cigarette into the flame. Sparks leapt, then died.

Sleep came in shifts, broken and thin. One man always watched while the others huddled close, the fire their tether to safety. Outside, the forest held its breath.

They were no longer just fugitives.

They were men caught in the teeth of winter, unsure of the trail ahead, bound together by necessity—and hunted not only by law, but by the wild that cared nothing for guilt or grace.

38

A cabin emerged from the trees like a promise —timbers dark against the snow, chimney leaning slightly with age. William slowed, eyes narrowing as he studied the familiar silhouette. Behind him, the others exhaled.

"Well, would you look at that," James muttered, relief threaded through disbelief. "A roof, real beds... maybe even something to eat."

Ethan grinned through a limp. "Better than frozen dirt."

William raised a hand. "Easy. Just because it's standing doesn't mean it's safe."

They approached with caution, the snow crunching beneath their boots loud in the hush. Inside, the air held the faint scent of old cedar and woodsmoke. Samuel swept through the rooms in silence, checking for movement, signs, anything.

Ethan wandered toward the kitchen, rifling through the cupboards with growing excitement. "Pantry's stocked. Looks like someone comes out here regular."

James sank onto a bunk with a groan. "These beds are better than any place we've been. Whoever owns this cabin? They know how to live."

William ignored them. "We don't settle in. Not really. We warm up, eat, rest, and plan. This isn't a safe house. It's a stopover."

He turned. "James—fire. Ethan, help."

As they worked, the cabin began to shift around them. Blankets were unrolled. A pot clanged in the kitchen. The hum of human activity returned to the quiet space like a heartbeat. Samuel came back in, shaking snow from his collar.

"No fresh tracks. Looks like we're alone for now."

James struck a match, hesitated. A photograph on the mantel caught his eye. He stepped closer.

A family. Framed in mid-laughter, years gone. And there, unmistakable in the back row—Sheridan.

"You guys..." he called out, voice suddenly flat. "Come see this."

Ethan and Samuel crowded in. Sheridan's face stared

back at them, younger, softer, but clear as day.

Ethan's stomach dropped. "No way."

"This is his," James said, voice dry. "We're in Sheridan's place."

Samuel's jaw tightened. The room felt smaller.

"Goddamn it," he muttered. "We're not just exposed— we're trespassing. If he's nearby..."

William took the photo, turned it slowly in his hands. "He's not just chasing us. We've stepped into his memory. This place is part of who he is."

Silence followed. Then William set the picture back, face down.

"We stay tonight. We're cold, hungry, and limping. But come first light, we move. Samuel, set a perimeter. James, keep that fire going. Ethan, help him."

There were no arguments.

As night came, the fire cracked and popped, pushing shadows into corners. Cans of stew were opened, their smell oddly comforting. For a moment, it felt like shelter.

Then the wolves began to howl.

Low. Distant. Closer than before.

James flinched. "That's... not far."

Ethan forced a laugh. "Sure. Just add wolves to the list."

Samuel, backlit by the window, didn't turn. "They're curious. That's all. But we keep the fire high. They don't like flames."

William nodded. "No chances. If they get too bold, we make noise. We scare them off. They won't fight unless they think they'll win."

They gathered closer to the warmth. The room tightened. Outside, darkness pressed against the glass, thick and absolute.

James murmured, "Still beats being out there."

Ethan nodded, rubbing his knee. "Even if Sheridan's on our tail, at least we've got walls."

Samuel smoked in silence, his face a flicker behind an orange glow.

Conversation faded. The fire dimmed to embers. One man kept watch while the others lay curled in borrowed warmth. The cabin held them, but it did not protect them.

They had taken shelter in the past of the man who hunted them. And the past had a way of catching up.

39

Sheridan's journey from the Ahanu home to the Old Prospector's trail was carved with grim resolve. The forest pressed in around him, branches skeletal with frost, the silence broken only by his own breath and the faint scuff marks that marked the fugitives' passage. Each print in the snow, each snapped twig, threaded him deeper toward the one place he had not expected to be threatened—his family's cabin.

At the base of a broad granite boulder, he crouched low. A burned-out campfire, ringed with disturbed earth, betrayed their recent presence. The tracks were hurried—dragged feet, shifting weight—no care taken to hide their movement. They were close. Too close.

A surge of fury rose in his chest. The cabin was no mere structure—it was memory. Laughter echoing off the porch. The smell of pancakes on slow mornings.

Summers folded into one another with bare feet and river swims. Now it was a waypoint for fugitives. His private world, breached.

As he climbed the ridge, a thin ribbon of smoke curled through the trees. The scent of it—pine and ash—coiled in his lungs. He slowed, eyes sharpening. There, just below, the cabin crouched against the riverbank, its chimney listing slightly, its windows faintly aglow.

He stopped at a thicket and parted the branches.

Movement. Shadows inside. Figures shifting.

A flicker of disbelief passed through him. They were already inside. Occupying the heart of his past like ghosts with bodies.

He didn't move. Didn't blink.

Instead, he melted back into the forest.

From a cleft among boulders a half-mile away, he found cover. A hollow known only to his children and himself—once a picnic spot, now a watchtower. It offered clear lines to the cabin, the woods, the trail back to the river. Strategic. Familiar.

Night bled into the canopy. The hush of the woods deepened. A wolf cried somewhere distant, and from the cabin came the murmur of raised voices.

They were fighting.

He listened.

The sounds were low but sharp—tension unraveling. That was good. Fractures made men careless.

He knelt in the dark, piecing his plan. He knew the layout of the cabin better than his own name: the narrow back window that opened with a firm shove, the loose board behind the stove, the slight squeak in the second floor's landing.

The moon, climbing, lit silver along the treetops. In its glow, he mapped the night.

Strike swift. Disorient. Separate.

He wouldn't charge in. He would bleed them dry—of confidence, of direction, of unity. Let their panic do half the work.

Every movement would matter. Every silence, too.

They were still arguing when he stood and turned back toward the cabin. The wind shifted. The firelight pulsed.

The trespassers had made themselves at home in his memories.

Now he would take them back.

40

His plan was meticulously crafted with the precision born of years in the wilderness. As dawn broke, casting a soft light through the dense canopy of trees, he set about constructing a heavy deadfall trap with a focus that left no room for error. His target was clear: to incapacitate one of the fugitives.

He chose a secluded spot along the path he anticipated one of the fugitives would take, near a natural choke point where the trail narrowed between thick brush and a large outcrop of rock. Here, he found a sizable log, heavy enough to ensure the trap's effectiveness yet manageable for him to maneuver into position with the use of levers and carefully placed stones for fulcrum points.

The trigger mechanism was simple yet ingenious, a

delicate balance of twigs and rope that would require minimal force to activate. He positioned the log so it teetered precariously, supported by the trigger stick, which, when disturbed, would release the log to fall with crushing force.

He then devised a trail of misleading signs: a few scattered belongings from his backpack, suggesting someone might have passed through in haste. He used branches to sweep the snow, creating a false trail leading directly to the deadfall trap. The psychological ploy was simple—prey upon the fugitives' desperation and curiosity, drawing them into the trap with the promise of supplies. He placed his backpack beneath the trap.

He concealed himself within a natural hideaway formed by dense foliage, with a clear view of the trap and the approach path. Patience was his ally as he waited, the slingshot ready by his side, a smooth stone nestled in the leather pouch.

Ethan stepped out into the cold, his breath visible in the crisp air. His initial reluctance gave way to a sense of purpose. Gathering firewood was a menial task, yet essential for their survival in the cabin's comforting warmth. "Just a quick trip," he muttered to himself, scanning the immediate vicinity, only to find the ground bare of any usable wood. With a sigh of resignation, he ventured further down a trail leading away from the cabin, his eyes peeled for any signs of firewood.

The discovery of a glove on the pristine snow sparked a trail of intrigue. Someone's been here, he mused, his curiosity piqued as he noticed more items—a scarf, a canteen, and a line of footprints—scattered ahead. Driven by the potential to find more than just firewood, he followed the makeshift breadcrumb trail, each item guiding him deeper into the woods.

Speculation whirled in his mind. Could someone else be out here? Lost? In trouble? These thoughts were interrupted as the trail led to an outcrop of rocks, where an abandoned backpack leaned. Approaching cautiously, half-expecting to confront someone, he peered inside. The backpack was filled with food and clothing—essential supplies that were too valuable to pass up in their desperate situation. Jackpot, he thought, a rush of relief momentarily easing his concerns.

Ethan's curiosity led him to a precarious discovery— a deadfall trap set up a few yards away from where he found the backpack. Constructed with a heavy log suspended ominously above the ground, it was a design he hadn't seen before. "What in the world?" he whispered, intrigued, overcoming his caution as he moved closer to inspect the primitive yet potentially lethal device.

His eyes carefully followed the setup, noting the trigger mechanism and the balance of the log. How does this even work? he wondered, both fascinated and unnerved by the ingenuity of the trap. His approach, a mix of curiosity and naiveté, brought him dangerously close to triggering it.

Hidden within the brush, Sheridan watched Ethan's every move with intense focus. Knowing the critical moment had arrived, he prepared his slingshot, taking aim at the trap's trigger mechanism. Tension palpable in his grip, he released the first shot. To his dismay, the stone veered off course, striking a nearby tree with a sharp crack.

The unexpected noise startled Ethan, who spun around, his heart racing as he scanned the forest. "Who's there?" he called out, the alarm in his voice slicing through the quiet of the woods. The break in silence echoed around him, heightening his alertness to the possibility that he was not alone in this secluded place.

Panicked but determined, Sheridan quickly loaded another stone into his slingshot. He couldn't afford to miss again. Ethan, momentarily distracted and looking in the wrong direction, didn't see Sheridan repositioning for another shot. Taking a deep breath to steady himself, he aimed and let the stone fly.

This time, his aim was perfect. The stone hit the trigger mechanism with a solid thud, releasing the heavy log suspended above. Ethan turned just in time to see the log crashing down towards him, his face registering shock and disbelief for a fleeting moment before the trap claimed him.

The forest fell silent once more, save for the echo of the trap's deadly clank. His heart pounding in his chest, Sheridan emerged from his hiding place, the reality of what he had done—and what he had been prepared to do—settling heavily upon him. He approached the scene with heavy steps. This was the grim measure he had taken to protect his family and his home. As he stood over the trap, he felt the weight of his actions deeply, a mix of relief and somber reflection on the necessity of such measures. It was a brutal testament to survival in the wilderness, a reminder of the stark decisions one must sometimes make in the face of danger.

The thunderous crash of the trap sent shockwaves through the men in the cabin, plunging them into a state of high alert. Samuel, seasoned in handling perilous situations, instinctively reached for his firearm, his movements precise and deliberate. Overtaken by panic, James began shouting for Ethan, but Samuel quickly silenced him with a stern look and a sharp gesture. "Quiet," he hissed, a grave tone to his voice. "We're not alone here."

As they carefully followed Ethan's tracks, the group rounded a bend and were confronted with a gruesome tableau. The massive log, now a grim instrument of death, lay sprawled across the narrow path, its weight having carved a deep impression in the snow. Beneath it, Ethan's body was visible, grotesquely pinned and mangled, the dark stain of his blood seeping into the white snow and painting the nearby boulders a stark, chilling red.

James' face drained of color, his shock manifesting as a physical tremor. "Ethan?" His voice cracked as it broke the eerie silence, the single word a plea laden with both hope and despair.

He surged forward, stumbling over snow-covered roots, dropping to his knees beside the log. "Ethan!" he cried again, grabbing at the unyielding weight of the trap. "Help me get it off him! We can still—" But even as he said it, the truth was writ in the stillness of Ethan's body.

From his vantage deep in the brush, Sheridan heard the screaming.

It wasn't just a cry of shock—it was grief cracking open in real time. The sound jolted through the trees, raw and unmistakably human, louder than the trap's collapse had been. It stopped Sheridan cold. He tightened his grip on the slingshot out of instinct, though there was no longer need for it. What struck him hardest wasn't the echoing voice—it was the name he heard torn from it. 'Ethan.'

Sheridan had no way of knowing which man it was. But in that voice, there was familiarity, love, disbelief. A brother, maybe. A friend. Someone who hadn't let go yet. Sheridan closed his eyes and listened to the grief, letting it settle into the folds of his conscience like cold rain into old stone.

This wasn't how he'd imagined it. He had hoped—if he had to act—that it would end with cold precision. That he could distance himself from the blood and call it strategy. Survival. But hearing the wail of a man broken open made it impossible. His hand dropped from the slingshot. His other touched the pouch on his hip, the one that had once carried dried berries for his daughter. His breath came slow, steady, but heavier now, edged with the weight of something irreversible.

He crouched deeper into the undergrowth, unseen, but no longer untouched. There would be no satisfaction in this. No righteous clarity. Only the hollow knowing that he had crossed a line—one he could never uncross—and the echo of a stranger's grief that would follow him long after the tracks were covered.

"James, stop," Samuel barked, his hand grabbing James by the collar and dragging him backward. "It's too late."

"Don't you touch me!" James snarled, struggling against Samuel's grip, his face contorted with rage and anguish. "You don't know that! He could still be breathing—"

"He's gone," William said firmly. "This trap wasn't meant to injure. It was meant to kill."

James collapsed into the snow, shaking with grief, his voice hoarse with disbelief. "This wasn't some accident. Someone did this... deliberately."

The sight was a brutal reminder of the dangers lurking in the wilderness—dangers that were now starkly personal and immediate. The trap, clearly not the work of an amateur, suggested a calculated intent that was horrifying in its efficiency. This was no accident—it was a message written in blood and snow; it was a meticulously set stage for murder, designed to kill with no chance for escape.

William's mind churned with questions and the bitter realization that they were not merely facing the dangers of the wilderness, but that they were being actively hunted. The cold dread settling in his stomach suggested they might indeed know who was targeting them. Samuel, his expression grim, noticed additional footprints that didn't belong to any of them. "This was no accident," he concluded, his voice low and menacing. "We're not just up against the elements anymore," he said tersely, his gaze scanning their surroundings for any further threats.

They retreated quickly to the cabin. James, visibly shaken, stumbled after them, his thoughts fixed on Ethan's fate. "Could it be Sheridan?" he muttered under his breath, his fear giving voice to the name that had been unspoken among them but haunting their every step. The heavy silence from William and Samuel confirmed his fears; they too harbored suspicions about Sheridan's involvement. The grim march back was filled with the echo of their hurried steps and the harsh breaths of men burdened by a harsh new reality.

As they settled back into the cabin, the air was thick with tension and the weight of their grim realization. Samuel immediately positioned himself by the window, his eyes scanning the shadowy tree line for any sign of movement. James was visibly shaken, sitting wrapped in a blanket, his shivering more from shock than cold. He rocked back and forth, muttering Ethan's name under his breath, sometimes louder, sometimes barely audible.

William paced back and forth, the wheels in his mind turning rapidly. "It could be Sheridan," he stated, pausing in his tracks. The name echoed ominously in the cramped space.

Looking over his shoulder, Samuel gave a grim nod. "He knows this land better than anyone. If he thinks we're threats..." His voice trailed off, the implication clear and chilling.

James, pale and distraught, suddenly exploded. "You don't know him! None of you do! He wouldn't—"

"He might," William cut in. "And we can't afford to assume otherwise."

There was a heavy silence as each man processed the

deadly new layer to their predicament. William finally stopped pacing and faced his companions squarely. "We need a plan," he declared firmly. "If Sheridan is setting traps, that means we're in his crosshairs. We stay here, fortify the cabin, and keep watch. No one goes out alone."

His orders were met with silent, grave nods; the severity of their situation was unmistakably clear.

The night stretched before them ominously, each sound from outside intensifying their anxiety—the wind's howl, a branch's snap—a constant reminder of the danger lurking just beyond their fragile refuge. Bound by necessity and a shared will to survive, the group prepared for a long, vigilant night.

They weren't just fugitives anymore.

They were prey.

41

U nder the shadowy veil of night, Sheridan's solitary camp was a stark, isolated spot pressed deep into the wild. Wrestling with the grim reality of his actions, he confronted emotions he hadn't expected. The idea of taking a life was alien, even now. But he had been driven by necessity—by a fierce, immovable need to protect his family, Ahanu's people, and the fragile peace carved from this land. The weight of that responsibility, while agonizing, steadied him. He would continue. He had to.

Meanwhile, tension churned through the cabin like a rising storm. James paced in short, restless bursts, voice raw with grief. "We can't just leave Ethan out there. We have to do something."

Samuel, standing at the window with a cigarette

burning low between his fingers, turned slowly. "James," he said, firm but not unkind, "the wolves have likely already found him. Going back puts us all at risk."

"He was one of us," James snapped, louder now. "You'd leave me too, wouldn't you?"

The words hung in the room like smoke. No one met his eyes.

William stood near the stove, arms crossed. "We have to prioritize staying alive."

James sank into a chair, shoulders tight, fists clenched. The silence afterward was thick, broken only by the crack of the stove.

Samuel exhaled smoke into the dim air. "We need to be smart—stay low, move fast. Fear can't call the shots."

William started gathering supplies. "At first light, we move east. Off-trail. It's rough ground, but better cover."

"And if he comes after us?" James's voice was hollow.

"We'll be ready," Samuel said.

As the night wore on, distant wolf howls threaded through the trees. The fire sank low, casting flickers across their worn faces. Ethan's fate hung in every pause. But there was no turning back. Not now.

Out in the darkness, Sheridan waited. He remained still as stone, breath shallow, eyes fixed on the cabin. He watched them leave one by one, their shapes cutting briefly through the pale wash of dawn —burdened, exhausted, unaware they were being marked. Only when the door thudded shut behind the last man and the fire inside dimmed to its final pulse did Sheridan move.

He slipped between the trees like dawn threading through the branches. Inside, the mess told the story —muddy prints, overturned chairs, crumbs of stolen food. The place was hollowed, its memory scuffed and discarded like a kicked stone.

But it was still his. And he would reclaim it.

He stood in the doorway, the pale dawn brushing across the floorboards like a slow exhale. Every memory here had been built with care: the shelves he carved, the beds he'd built, the stones he'd placed just so around the fire. All of it, violated.

He would follow. Not out of vengeance. This wasn't personal. It was protection. He would contain the threat.

He tracked them silently—an echo without a sound. His snowshoes whispered over the powder, smooth and effortless. In contrast, the fugitives blundered forward, boots punching through snow, breath loud, shoulders sagging.

Nearly eight hours passed. Then William raised a hand and pointed to a clearing hemmed in by spruce.

"Here. We camp."

James let out a groan, his knees buckling slightly as he dropped his pack. "Finally."

Samuel didn't pause. He swung a hatchet from his belt and started clearing a space. "We need a fire. Otherwise, we freeze."

William turned. "James—wood. Kindling. Now."

James hesitated, glancing toward the trees. "Won't a fire give us away?"

William's jaw tensed. "So will our frozen bodies."

"But what if he's still out there?" James's voice dropped. "Watching?"

Samuel didn't look up from where he crouched over the fire pit. "He's out there."

James blinked. "You saw him?"

"Didn't have to," Samuel said. He paused, testing the air. "I know when I'm being watched."

James shifted his weight. "So we're just gonna sit here and wait to get picked off?"

William stepped in, voice tight. "We sit in the dark, we die slower. You want to freeze, or burn?"

Samuel finally met James's gaze. "He won't strike tonight. Not while we're expecting him."

James let out a slow breath, shoulders sagging. Then he turned and stepped toward the trees, each footfall louder than it needed to be.

The forest pressed in. Every sound—a branch creak, a squirrel's chatter—made him flinch.

Back at the fire ring, Samuel looked to William. "We'll take turns. Every two hours."

William nodded. "Agreed."

They lit a modest fire. Flames danced and threw jagged shadows across their faces. They huddled in, drawn to the light, but afraid of what it invited.

A lone wolf howled in the distance. No one spoke.

Samuel took the first watch. He stood like a sentry, unmoving, while the others drifted into shallow, broken sleep.

And still, Sheridan watched. From the darkness, he studied the glow of their fire—the fragile orange heartbeat of trespassers. His eyes never left them.

He touched the hilt of his knife. Not for courage. For memory.

The line had been drawn.

He would let them rest.

But come morning, the forest would remember who had always belonged to it.

42

Dawn crept slowly over the ridge, a pale wash of light that softened nothing. Sheridan moved with purpose, every step deliberate, every sound weighed. His breath coiled in the cold, thin air as he climbed, searching not just for elevation but for position—somewhere they would have no choice but to pass.

He found it where the forest narrowed—a natural funnel pressed between a steep rise and a thicket of twisted spruce. A windfallen tree leaned nearby, its trunk thick and gnarled, its branches clawing at the air. It would do.

He worked in silence. The rope burned against his fingers as he fashioned the rigging, knotting it cleanly, tightly. The log was heavy with age, water-soaked, its bark worn bald in places. He tested its swing with the tension of a hunter's patience. It hung now, still and ready, a blunt answer to intrusion.

Near the base of the path, he set a line—a tripwire thin as a bramble root, nearly invisible against the frost-bitten debris. Across from it, he crouched low in the brush, shaping stakes from broken limbs, each one carved to a point and pressed deep into the earth. There was no rage in it, only calculation. No hatred, only duty. He buried them beneath a bed of needles and snow, their presence hidden to all but the trees.

When it was done, he didn't linger. He backed away slowly, leaving no prints to betray his position. From the slope above, he watched the trail. Waited.

Below, the men were stirring. Ash clung to the rim of their fire pit, but the warmth was gone. They stood stiffly, rubbing hands over arms, stretching cold limbs. The weight of the forest had pressed on them all night.

"We need to move," William said, voice hoarse. "East. Tight formation."

Samuel nodded, the cigarette in his mouth unlit but clenched like a ritual. "He'll have laid traps."

James hovered at the edge of the group, silent until now. "What if we hit one?"

William slung his pack over his shoulder. "Then we deal with it."

James stared at the trees. "And if we don't see it coming?"

"We won't," Samuel said. "That's the point."

They began to walk. No one spoke again for a while. The forest had teeth, and they all felt its breath.

Each step was hesitant. Every root and rock was a suspect. William moved like a man trying to walk between raindrops. Samuel's gaze swept the underbrush in wide arcs. James trailed behind, arms tight against his chest, the air thick with what none of them would say.

A squirrel burst from a bush and darted across their path. James flinched hard.

"You hear that?" he whispered.

"Just nerves," William muttered.

But no one relaxed.

Up ahead, hidden among the shadows, Sheridan waited. He saw them before they saw him—figures trudging, heads low, feet careless with fatigue.

He let his hand rest on the hilt of his knife.

Not yet.

Let them pass. Let the wire sing.

He watched the wind play through the branches overhead, the trap swaying slightly like a pendulum measuring time.

And time, he knew, was nearly up.

The shadowed trail seemed to draw them deeper into an ominous wilderness, far removed from any semblance of safety. William's voice, stern and laden with urgency, cut through the silence. "Stay sharp, and stay close. We're not alone in these woods."

James, still reeling from the loss of Ethan and the weight of it all, lagged behind.

"James, for God's sake, keep up! Don't drift away—it's what he wants."

Jolted, James caught up, but his grief and distraction saw him inadvertently take the lead.

"Something's not right," Samuel muttered. His hand hovered at his hip. The woods felt too quiet, the silence thick and unnatural.

A metallic whisper sliced through the air—a soft click, almost nothing.

Samuel lunged forward. "James! Down—"

But it was too late.

The log came swinging out of the trees like a judgment. It hit James full in the chest, lifted him clean off the ground, and flung him into the thicket. There was the sickening crack of wood, the sharper sound of something breaking—and then silence. A lone crow burst from the canopy, its wings scraping the air like a curse, and somewhere deep in the woods, a tree groaned in the wind as if bearing witness.

William and Samuel ran.

The underbrush parted to reveal James, skewered on a bed of sharpened stakes. Blood trickled down the wooden points in slow, glistening ribbons, dripping onto the snow where it sizzled faintly against the frost. Steam lifted like a ghost from the wound, curling into the cold morning air.

His eyes were wide but empty—fixed on nothing, already beyond reach.

Samuel stood frozen. For a breath, the forest held still, as if stunned by its own cruelty.

Then he roared, his voice raw, the sound tearing from some deep place of rage and grief. "Sheridan! You bastard!" He fired into the trees, one shot, two, three—wild and echoing. "You hear me? You've taken everything!"

William grabbed his arm. "Stop. He's watching. We need to move. Now."

Samuel resisted. His gun wavered in his grip, but his voice broke. "He was just a kid."

"We'll make it count," William said, quieter now. "But not here."

They backed away, dragging their pain with them.

Sheridan, perched high in the trees, didn't move. His chest ached. Not from cold, but from what he had done. He whispered to no one, "I'm sorry, James."

He hadn't wanted this. He wanted safety. He wanted his family to sleep without fear. But this was the price of wanting, and the forest had collected.

Down below, Samuel trudged forward in silence, rage now a quiet boil. Butte felt far away. The city, the noise, the dirt—all of it reduced to ghosts in these woods. James had been loud there, reckless, loyal. A brother, almost. His death cleaved something open.

'This isn't what I signed up for,' he thought. But he knew now—he wouldn't walk away empty. Not this time.

"I'll make it right," he muttered. "I swear."

William kept his eyes forward. Each loss was a stone added to his back, but he carried them. Chicago had taught him to lead. Here, leadership meant survival, even if it came stained in red.

Above, Sheridan's breath came slow. He watched them retreat. Then he turned away.

There was still more to come.

The forest held its breath.

43

The snow crunched beneath their boots, brittle and loud in the quiet of the forest. Each footfall seemed to echo with accusation, as if the trees themselves bore witness to what had just happened. William and Samuel moved quickly, their bodies hunched, breath coming sharp and fast in the cold air. No words passed between them at first—just the sting of wind, the rhythm of survival.

At last, Samuel broke. "Fuck! How the hell did he know we'd come this way?"

His voice cracked the hush like a rifle report. Rage surged beneath the surface, but fear ran deeper. He was no stranger to violence, but this—this was something else. Being hunted, outmaneuvered, undone at every turn. It felt personal.

William didn't stop. "He knows this land like it's his

own breath. We're not chasing him—we're dancing to his tune."

His tone wasn't bitter, just brutally clear. He was already recalibrating, thinking in lines of defense, angles, escape routes.

"We need to stop reacting," he said. "We need to make him come to us."

Samuel exhaled, long and hard. "You want to turn and fight."

"I want to stop bleeding men."

They kept moving, eyes on the terrain, ears tuned to the creak of limbs and the low moan of wind threading through the trees. The silence was oppressive. The woods felt as though they were folding in around them.

Eventually, Samuel spoke again. "We find high ground. Clear sightlines. Nothing at our back but stone."

William gave a short nod. "And we hold."

There was no illusion of safety—only a sliver of strategy. But strategy, at least, felt like something they could still control.

Sheridan watched them from the ridgeline. They were close now—worn thin, but not yet broken. He tracked them with the patience of someone who had learned not just to hunt, but to wait.

Then he saw it.

Movement to his right.

He stilled.

From between the trees stepped a wolf—large, gray, its coat thick and weather-touched. It regarded him without fear, its eyes neither hostile nor tame. For a breathless moment, man and animal simply looked at each other.

Sheridan didn't reach for his weapon.

The wolf turned its head, ears flicking toward a shadowed path that wound deeper into the woods. It held his gaze a moment longer, then moved off, silent as mist.

He stood rooted.

It was the same wolf, he was sure of it. The one from the shoreline days ago. Miakoda's words surfaced in his mind: *'Wolves are the old ones. They know what we forget.'*

A sign? A warning? Or just an animal obeying its nature?

He stepped lightly after it.

There was no trail—only instinct. The wolf didn't lead in a straight line, but its presence guided him nonetheless. Through brush and bramble, over frost-hardened soil, he moved with the same deliberate grace he used when stalking elk. But this wasn't prey. This was something else.

Not a chase. Not a trap. An alignment.

The fugitives' path reemerged ahead—bootprints etched into thin snow, broken twigs, a discarded scrap of cloth.

The wolf was gone now.

But Sheridan moved forward with clearer eyes. Not just a protector now, not only a man avenging trespass. Something in him had shifted. The forest wasn't a backdrop—it was an ally. The silence, the wind, the wolf—they were with him.

And he was no longer following men. He was answering something older. Something that called not from rage, but from the bones of the land.

A breeze stirred, and with it came the faint scent of pine sap and woodsmoke—remnants of their passage. A raven called out overhead, harsh and singular, and in his chest, something settled. A knowing. A vow.

He stepped forward, the snow crunching softly beneath his boot.
And the forest exhaled with him.

44

The snow-crusted clearing opened before them, stark and unforgiving. Beyond it, the frozen lake stretched like a sheet of hammered glass —silent, vast, and deadly. The shift from dense forest to this barren plain was jarring, as though they'd stepped into another world. William scanned the terrain, eyes sharp.

"Stay alert, Samuel. This might be our best shot at putting distance between us and Sheridan," he said, his breath ghosting in the air.

The ice shimmered with treachery. It offered speed —but at a cost. William weighed each step, the way a commander reads a battlefield. The exposure made his skin crawl, but the urgency of pursuit left no choice.

"We're exposed, but it's faster than going around. We

move quick, keep low," he muttered. The cold stung his lungs, the burden of leadership pressing harder with every decision.

Samuel's gaze swept the treeline. "Stick to the edge. Harder to track us. But he's out there. Watching."

Their boots crunched as they moved—no cover, no shadows, just brittle sound and breath. Above, a raven cried, its call skimming across the lake like a warning.

They reached the lake's edge. Then it happened.

Samuel's foot caught. A groan of snow. The crack of branches giving way.

And he was gone.

"William!"

A pit. Sharpened stakes. The thud of flesh against wood. William dropped to his knees, heart slamming.

Samuel lay impaled, eyes wide with shock, blood blooming around the stakes. "Hold on!" William shouted, already tearing at his sack.

With a grunt of effort, he climbed down into the pit, boots slipping in blood and snow. He braced Samuel's torso, teeth gritted. "I have to lift you. This is going to hurt."

Samuel's lips trembled. "Do it."

William gripped him and pulled. The stakes gave a sickening groan as Samuel's body slid free, blood spilling anew. Samuel screamed—raw, guttural, human.

William dragged him out and laid him in the snow, hands instantly working to stop the bleeding. Tourniquets, cloth, pressure. The snow turned red beneath them, steam rising from the wound.

Samuel coughed, gasped. "Got a smoke?"

William stared at him, stunned. Then—fumbling—he found the pack in his coat. Shaky fingers drew one out, lips pressing it between Samuel's bloodied lips.

"You lightin' it or not?" Samuel croaked.

William struck a match, shielding the flame with his hand. He lit the cigarette and watched as Samuel inhaled, the ember flaring against the cold.

"Christ," Samuel whispered, smoke curling from his lips. "Hurts like hell."

William pressed harder on the wound. "You're not dying here."

"Not planning to," Samuel said, but his voice was thinner now. "I just... needed something."

Then—a sound.

Low. Guttural. The crackle of branches underfoot.

William's head snapped up. Wolves.

Emerging from the trees, their eyes gleamed. Gray

coats, breath puffing white in the cold. They moved with purpose. Predatory grace.

Samuel stiffened. "No. No. Not like this."

William's hands hovered, caught between pressure and pistol.

The wolves stepped closer.

"William," Samuel said, voice barely audible. "Please."

William's heart slammed in his chest. Every instinct screamed to run—but Samuel's eyes held him.

"I can't... I'm sorry."

William backed away, steps faltering. Samuel's cigarette slipped from his fingers, extinguished in the snow.

"Don't leave me to them!" Samuel's cry rose, echoing across the clearing.

But William ran.

From the shadows, Sheridan watched.

He had not meant this.

The pit had been meant to warn, not wound. The wolves—drawn by scent and desperation—were not his weapon, but they had become part of his war. Now, as the pack slinked from the brush with low growls and hungry eyes, Sheridan saw the edges of his choices fray into something unrecognizable.

Samuel's broken voice rang out. "You did this!"

Sheridan stepped from the treeline, slow and hollow-eyed. Not a soldier now. Not a hunter. Just a man bearing the weight of decisions that had outpaced their meaning.

He met Samuel's gaze—and faltered.

There was no hatred in the young man's face, only fear. Raw, primal. A soul laid bare in its final moments. Sheridan felt it punch through him, that unspoken plea. The recognition that this wasn't justice. It was abandonment.

He opened his mouth but found no words. What apology could unmake this? What comfort could he offer while the wolves circled like shadows made flesh?

This was not the way.

The land had taught him patience, taught him how to endure. But it had never taught him how to carry this kind of regret. His traps had never wept. His quarry had never asked for mercy.

He took one step forward—and stopped.

Too late.

The wolves advanced, slow and deliberate, eyes gleaming with an old hunger.

Sheridan's fists curled at his sides. He had aimed

to protect his people, to outmatch his enemies with cunning and restraint. But somewhere along the path, he had become something else—something colder, more calculated. And now the land he loved had mirrored that savagery back at him.

"This was never the way," he whispered.

A cold gust swept across the clearing. The cigarette, now dark, tumbled and rolled in the snow.

The trees bore silent witness.

And the wilderness, indifferent and eternal, reclaimed what was hers.

45

In the vast, unyielding quiet of the northern wilderness, where the only witnesses were ancient pines and the endless expanse of snow, the final confrontation between William and Sheridan unfolded—a stark, defining moment that would seal their fates in the heart of the cold, indifferent forest.

William stood on the frozen lake, gun in hand, pointed at Sheridan. A myriad of thoughts raced through his mind. The isolation of the Alberta wilderness, so far removed from the life he once controlled in Chicago and Butte, underscored the gravity of his situation. He was no longer the orchestrator but a player in a game dictated by survival, wit, and the merciless laws of nature.

The wolves, scattered by Sheridan's approach, became distant shadows, their presence a reminder of the wild's indifference to human affairs. He walked with measured steps, emanating a calmness born of necessity and understanding. His gaze, steady and unyielding, met William's with an intensity that spoke volumes. In this desolate landscape, their confrontation was not just a clash of wills but a profound dialogue of existence.

"What are you going to do, William?" His voice carried across the cold air, a direct challenge. "You think pulling that trigger changes anything? We're both just men trying to protect what's ours."

William's arm, though steady, felt the weight of his gun as if it were a leaden anchor, dragging him down into the abyss of his own making. The realization that Sheridan, the man he had seen as an adversary, was driven by the same primal forces of protection and survival, began to erode the walls of hostility he had built.

"I... I was just trying to survive," he said. The words felt more like a confession than a justification. But at what cost? The gun in his hand, once a symbol of control and power, now felt like a testament to his failures and losses.

"Survival doesn't have to mean losing who we are," Sheridan said. "We make choices. It's those choices that define us, not the wilderness, not the gun in our hand."

On the frozen expanse under the vast Alberta sky,

they stood not as adversaries but as reflections of each other, each confronting the cost of their choices.

William lowered his gun. The act felt like a surrender, not to Sheridan, but to the futility of the conflict. "I'm tired, Sheridan. Tired of running, tired of fighting." His voice, barely above a whisper, marked the end of a long, harrowing journey.

Sheridan stepped closer, offering a nod. "Let's end this cycle, William. There's more to survival than just staying alive. It's about what we're living for."

The two men, once bound by a cycle of pursuit and survival, found themselves at a crossroads. The choice to lower the gun opened a path to redemption—a fragile understanding.

Then, the ice cracked.

The frozen lake groaned beneath them, the sound rising like a warning, then split with a violent crack. William plunged into the freezing abyss.

"No!" Sheridan shouted, horror overtaking him. The brittle silence of the forest shattered. Every instinct honed by years of living with the land propelled him forward.

Scrambling for anything, Sheridan found a long branch. "William, grab on!" he called, extending the branch across the precarious ice.

William, his hands numb, fumbled toward the lifeline. His struggle was against more than just the water—it was against the weight of his past. At last, his fingers found the branch, and Sheridan, teeth gritted, pulled with all his strength.

The ice groaned. Inch by inch, William was dragged free, until he collapsed on solid ground, soaked and shivering. Sheridan wrapped him in his blanket, his breath fogging in the frigid air.

Lying there, William gazed up at the sky. It was not the cold that overwhelmed him now, but the realization that he had been given a second chance.

Sheridan stood over him, the branch still in hand —a symbol now of mercy, not war. "Survival," he murmured, "is about more than just living through another day. It's about what we live for."

A few steps away, the remains of Samuel lay stark in the snow.

William's face twisted in grief. Gratitude and rage warred within him. As Sheridan turned, a shadow crossed William's heart. He stood, his muscles aching, and leveled the gun at Sheridan's back.

"You saved me," he said, voice cracking. "But you took everything from me. My friends... Ethan, James, Samuel. You turned our escape into a nightmare."

Sheridan turned slowly. "I did what I thought was necessary," he said quietly. "To protect my family. My land. But this—" he gestured to the snow, the broken bodies, "this was never the intention."

"Killing me won't bring them back," he added. "We've both lost. It's over."

"It's never over!"

An arrow flew.

It struck William clean through the right eye. He fell back into the snow, gun firing once into the air.

Sheridan spun to see Ahanu at the treeline, bow in hand, another arrow already nocked. The sight of his old friend brought a sharp breath to his chest.

"Sheridan!" Ahanu called, racing forward. "You all right?"

He nodded, shaken but alive. Ahanu's presence, quiet and resolute, was a balm.

Ahanu stepped closer, eyes locking with Sheridan's. "This land binds us. It's worth fighting for. Worth protecting."

Sheridan nodded, emotion tightening his throat. "Thank you, Ahanu."

Together, they faced the aftermath, united in purpose. The wilderness, harsh and beautiful, was their home. They would guard it, live with it, learn from it.

Then came the sound of hooves. Mountie McFee emerged from the trees, followed by Frank Jackson and two more officers. From another path came his sons, Michael and David, their faces pale but determined.

Sheridan stood among them—family, friends, and those who had seen it all.

In the fading light, with the sky brushed in hues of gold and crimson, the weight of everything settled around him. The violence, the loss, the choices. But also the resilience, the unity, and the chance to begin again.

This was not just the end.

It was the beginning of something new.

Here, among those he loved, he would rebuild. Here, at the edge of the wild, he would remember that home is not just a place, but the people who stand with you when the storm is past.

The wilderness had been his crucible.

Now, it would be his sanctuary.

THE END

DJ ATKINSON

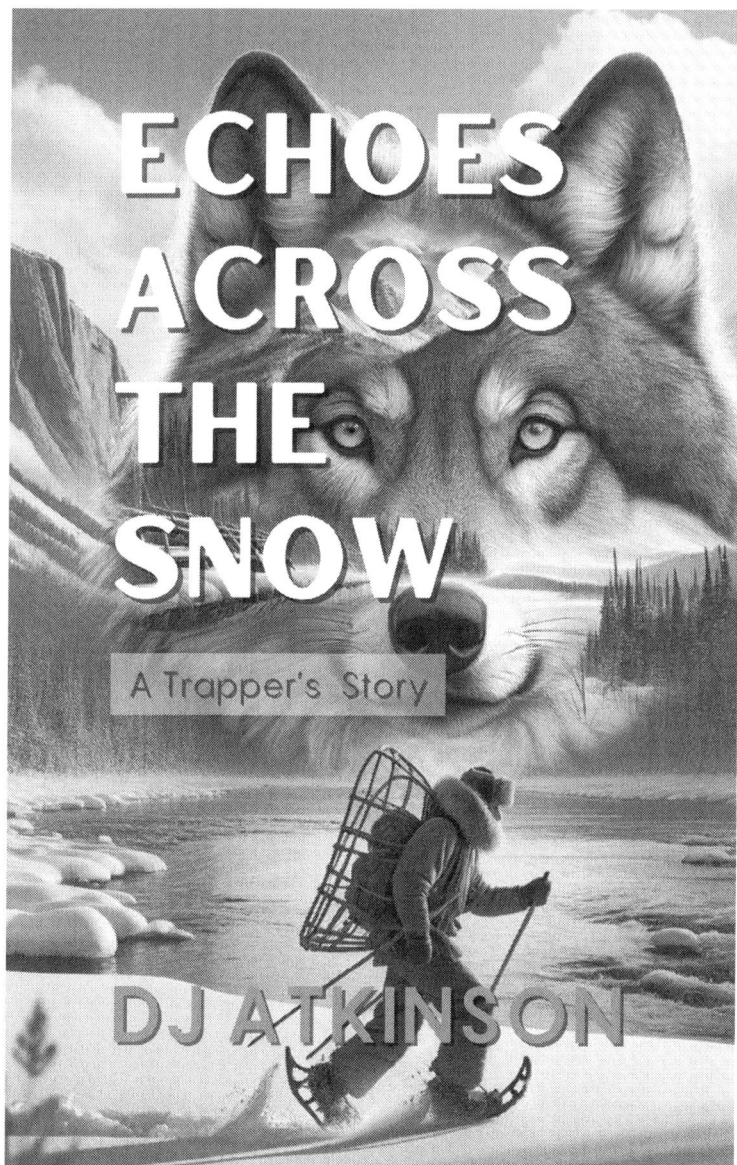

ECHOES
ACROSS
THE
SNOW

A Trapper's Story

DJ ATKINSON

About the Author

In 'Echoes Across the Snow', DJ Atkinson's second novel. He is renowned for his rich, intricate narratives that explore the human condition against the backdrop of severe, often unforgiving environments. Atkinson's writing is distinguished by its deep psychological insight and vivid descriptive power, drawing readers into the world he crafts with an immersive intensity. His characters are meticulously developed, each embodying a complex blend of strengths and vulnerabilities that reflect the broader human experience.

In his narratives, Atkinson delves into the complexities of survival, not just in the physical sense but also on a moral and spiritual level. His characters are frequently placed in extreme situations that compel them to confront their deepest fears and moral dilemmas, challenging their preconceived notions of right and wrong. This exploration often culminates in themes of redemption, resilience, and the transformative power of nature, which acts both as a harsh judge and a redemptive force.

Atkinson's works pose significant questions about the essence of humanity and the potential for personal growth in the face of adversity. Through his vivid storytelling, he underscores the importance of community, family, and the unyielding human spirit, making his books not only compelling narratives but also profound studies of life's enduring challenges.

Books by DJ Atkinson

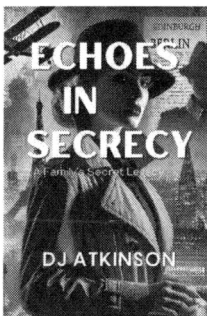

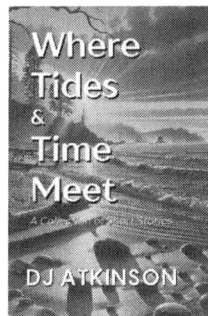

Manufactured by Amazon.ca
Bolton, ON

46588917R00144